Because Of My Love For Lauren

By LaVina Vanorny-Barcus

LaVina Vanorny Barcus

Copyright ©2010 by LaVina Vanorny-Barcus
Published in the USA
No part of this book may be reproduced in any form or by electronic or mechanical means, including information storage and retrieval systems, without written permission from LaVina Vanorny-Barcus.

All of the characters and situations in this book are fictitious and only exist in the imagination of the author and have no relationship what so ever to anyone bearing the same name or characteristics.

Chapter One

When Robert Jones woke up he had to pry his eyes open. He instantly squeezed them tightly shut and rubbed them with both fists until he cleared his vision. The bright sunlight streaming through the slits between the blinds caused a stab of pain behind his eyes and lower forehead. What was he drinking? Oh yeah…Crown Royal and Coke. It always caused a hangover that lasted most of the next day. Somehow he always convinced himself, each time he was tempted, that this time the outcome would be different.

The mound of blankets moved on the king size bed beside him. He peeked under the corner of the blue plaid comforter to reveal the back of a female head covered with long red hair. He'd wake her up but frankly he couldn't remember her name. Oh well, hopefully she'd wake up and exit the house quietly so he wouldn't have to face her.

She wasn't anything special, but she was willing to come home with him and the hour had been late. Again, Crown Royal and Coke was quite a persuader and had done its job.

He swung his muscular legs off of the side of the bed with a deep sigh. He searched the oak bed stand through puffed up eyes for the bottle of acetaminophen. He kept it handy, since lately it had become his morning routine. He dumped three into his hand and swallowed them without water. He stood up, put his hands on his lower back and stretched.

He caught sight of his image in the huge dresser mirror. Even with a hangover he was a striking figure. He had thick wavy hair with a distinguished touch of gray. He had big blue eyes with dark lashes and few wrinkles. He had a strong jaw line, perfect teeth and worked very hard to keep muscular and fit.

Women liked the fact that he was six foot three and always dressed to the hilt. Expensive Italian suits and leather designer shoes were monthly purchases for him. He always bought at least two ties to go with every shirt he owned. Sometimes he would change several times before he left the house to go to work to get just the right look for the clients of that day. The fact that he was a widower and had never had children also seemed to please the ladies, less baggage for them to deal with is how he figured it.

A steaming hot shower is just what he needed. He quickly dropped his royal blue boxers and stepped in onto the wet tile floor, closing the green striped curtain behind him.

The hot water felt shocking at first and made him gasp. After it beat on the top of his head for a few minutes he felt some needed relief. His head was slowly clearing.

He heard the bedroom door open, then shut and smiled. Good…she was gone. It was so awkward to be forced to make small talk the morning after when you both knew you regretted the decisions of the night before.

Suddenly, he felt the cramps starting under the edge of his rib cage. He fought it for a moment, then flung the fabric shower curtain open and fell to his knees in front of the white porcelain toilet. The waves of convulsions continued until his stomach was empty. Crown Royal and Coke tasted so bitter the second time around.

This had been happening for five to six weeks now. He guessed it was time to make a doctor appointment, though he laughed to himself that all the doctors ever told him to do was to stop drinking. Fat chance! Drinking definitely added to his humor and charm and was important in the games he played with the women he met.

Just the thought of drinking Crown and Coke started his stomach to churn and he dropped to his knees by the toilet for one more round.

Chapter Two

Doctor Gene Kimball was a tall, slightly built man with heavy framed glasses that slid down the bridge of his nose each time he looked down at the dull black clipboard. His dark hair was very thick and was streaked with shades of gray. He now wore it combed straight back to camouflage the fact that his hair was thinning at the crown, though it also kept it out of his way while he examined his patients.

Robert Jones sized up the man sitting in front of him. He was sure he made good money but he didn't look like he knew how to enjoy himself. He probably ate healthy food, worked out and was asleep by 11:00 every night. What a waste of a man with plenty of bucks in his pocket.

"I have your test results back," Dr. Kimball said. "I think we have identified the problem."

The doctor's voice was so monotonous that Robert Jones had to force himself to focus on what the boring man was saying.

"I'm sorry to tell you that your test results indicate that you have Hepatocellular

Carcinoma or commonly it's referred to as cancer of the liver." He paused and looked down. Again the glasses had to be pushed back up into place. "We need to start a vigorous plan of chemotherapy as soon as possible. Your future depends on it"

Robert Jones was speechless! Had he heard correctly? How could such a vital man such as himself, have cancer? He worked out several times a week and was very proud of his strength. He was only fifty four years old and was at the height of his career as a chemical salesman. He was the envy of most men he knew! He had women coming out of the woodwork to spend time with him. Some of them were half his age. He had not expected anything like this.

Through a fog, he received instructions on what clinic to go to get his treatments and what side effects he should expect. He sat there with a confused look on his face, shaking his head from side to side slowly in disbelief.

"I know this is hard to accept but we must move on your treatment quickly." The doctor stated. "We will help you through this," he continued. "Medical science has made many advances and I will personally monitor all of your test results. All test results will go directly to me. N o one else will even see them so there won't be any confusion." He smiled reassuringly and lowered his voice saying, "Don't worry. I will take good care of you."

They shook hands and he walked out of the office. How ironic he thought as he expertly wove his Mercedes in and out of the heavy traffic. He had finally gotten his life together again and now had to face this. He had earned lots of money and could buy the best care available. Doctor Kimball was considered a leading specialist in the field and had certificates all over his walls to prove it. He came very highly recommended from others in the medical professions..

Robert wasn't going to sweat it. He'd handle this just like he handled difficult customers. He'd make them realize that he was not a person to mess with. If Doctor Kimball says he will personally monitor his testing and treatment then Robert *would* hold him to his word or he would raise hell until he did.

You don't promise something to Robert Jones and not deliver.

Chapter Three
Chemo-The First Round

What a process. What a waste of a day. Robert was scheduled to start his treatments at 10:00 a.m. but he had to be there at 8:30 a.m. for blood tests first. This would be his routine for the next twenty Mondays. Doctor Kimball said due to possible side effects he would have to come to the hospital in a taxi cab. The chemo process would take a total of about four hours. The blood tests would determine the rest.

How boring to have to sit there for four hours. He was a busy man with important things to do. When you are paid with commissions, every minute counts and could equal a larger paycheck. He could not risk his career, but like the doctor said, "If you don't have a life, a career isn't worth very much."

His nurse stopped in the doorway. "How are you doing?" she asked with her long lashes framing her huge blue eyes. "Do you feel sick to your stomach?"

"No," he replied. "I'm just bored to death."

"I'm sorry about that," she said. He decided she was about thirty years old but still real pretty with her long blonde hair tied up into a pony tail. She was a tiny petite woman with narrow hips and a full bust line. She wore light blue scrubs that fit loose and baggy but he could still see she was shapely and physically fit underneath.

"I wish I could help but all I have to offer is this TV set." She used the remote control to turn it on and said, "Is there a channel that you would like to watch?"

"Whatever's on is fine. I'm usually working so I don't know a lot about shows on TV." Personally he thought most TV shows were for brain dead people that had nothing exciting or worth while in their own lives and wanted excitement from stories about other people. In particular he hated the morbid commercials that rotated over and over as each hour went by. He guessed that working in sales caused him a hatred of being sold to.

If there was a plus side to this whole thing it may have been having her as his nurse. He was apprehensive when he arrived but she explained everything as she was doing it and it made him relax. As she drew the blood for the lab testing, she explained in that sweet, but oh so calm, voice, that it would always be a two-step process. Drawing blood, waiting for the results directly from Dr Kimball, and if Robert's immune system was handling the chemicals sufficiently they would then start the chemo intravenously.

"Now you'll feel a pinch," she said. She inserted a thin needle into the vein on the top of his left hand that was swathed in iodine.

"Ow!!" Robert yelled. Though, as soon as he spoke the discomfort from the pinch was gone.

"I'm sorry I hurt you," she said leaning closer. He could smell her floral perfume and decided she was a nice distraction to what he was going through. She attached a thin plastic tube that was about the size of a fat spaghetti noodle to the end of the needle.

A grinding screech was heard as she pulled a metal IV stand over by him and hung a clear plastic bag of liquid from one of the hooks.

"The wheels on these things need oil badly." she said laughing. "Oh well," she continued. "It's usually worth a chuckle or two!" She flashed him a huge smile and he decided he was right. Things could always be worse.

"Robert," he said extending his free hand. "Robert Jones."

"Well hello, Robert Jones." She offered her hand to him. "I'm Maria Anderson."

"Maria," He gestured to his arm loaded with the needle, tubes and strips of white tape. "Can you speed up this process?"

"I'm sorry," she answered. "There's nothing I can do about the drip rate. Your body can only handle the chemo so fast. You are also being injected with a very powerful form of chemo. It is three times as strong as most patients receive. But hopefully that means you'll recover three times faster."

Robert looked at the confusion of plastic tubing and saw it had filled with a clear liquid and it was slowly moving down toward the needle in his hand.

She smiled apologetically and headed out of the door. The bounce of her pony tail suddenly made him smile and he closed his eyes.

Robert Jones was sitting at a sticky wooden table with a tall foamy glass of beer. It was 1977 and his college days were almost over since he would graduate in May. He was celebrating his acceptance of his dream job.

When he was interviewing for jobs he really didn't care what the job position was, it just had to have high pay and opportunities to make big bucks in commissions and chances for promotions. It also needed to impress people so they would think it was an important job.

The job he landed was with a large successful Fortune 500 company and a lot of prestige came with the position. Many of his college classmates interviewed for this same job but in the end his determination and air of confidence proved itself. He would even start at a higher base wage then he expected.

He would be selling a new chemical that his company just received the patent for. The entire deal just reeked of opportunity, plus would be very lucrative.

Robert vowed never to live an average life. He liked big houses and fast expensive cars and he wasn't going to settle for anything less or let anyone stand in his way.

When he was a senior in high school he received an inheritance from his Grandmother. The money was used to pay for his college education. What was left, he used to buy a Firebird Trans Am, bright red, with a black firebird decal covering the hood. His car turned the heads of many young women, which was the plan from the beginning. He quickly got the reputation of being a lady's man and a player, something he was quite proud of.

As he chugged the last of his beer a silky blonde pony tail caught his eye out on the dance floor. The blonde was in the arms of a thin fraternity brother with dark rimmed glasses. Definitely a geek, Robert thought, and as the young man turned he could see his pocket protector filled with mechanical pencils and a yellow highlighter. No surprise.

Robert sat watching her blonde pony tail sway from side to side to the beat of the slow music. Something the thin boy said must have been amusing because she suddenly smiled. Her eyes crinkled and lit up with excitement. Robert instantly knew he would have to meet her.

The spring Sigma Nu fraternity dance was the event of the year. She was one of the *few freshman girls that had been asked. Having the invitation come from a senior was even more exciting plus they had been friends since the beginning of the school year.*

She was majoring in Fashion Merchandising and she designed the dress she was wearing for one of her classes. The dress fit her narrow waist perfectly and the deep rust color accented her green eyes and her olive skin. The DJ was playing many of her favorite songs. Her date was somewhat shy, but their conversations had been lively. He was very nice and treated her like a queen. The night was perfect.

Robert knew the thin young man was no competition for him. He stood up, feathered back his dark hair with his comb and headed right out onto the wooden dance floor. He walked up to the girl, skillfully slipped her hand from her dates hand and stepped in between them. He took her other hand and in a flash she was dancing with Robert as Robert danced with his back to her date. She started to object but he could tell she was flattered.

"I only dance with very beautiful women," he said as he looked her up and down. "And you are by far the most

beautiful woman in the room." He pulled her close so she would have to follow his lead, and he guided her to the other side of the dance floor. Robert looked over his shoulder and saw that the young man was still standing there in the dim shadows, with his arms at his sides, not sure what to do next. Finally the jilted party shook his head, and quite defeated he walked back to his table of frat brothers.

She blushed from Robert's attention, "I need to go back to my date now." She protested. "He's my ride home."

"Not any more," and Robert twirled her around and pulled her back tightly against him with confidence. He looked deep into her eyes until she felt she was swallowed up in their darkness.

"Hi, I'm Robert, Robert Jones." He stepped away and bowed gallantly.

"I'm Lauren," she said timidly. "Lauren Powers." Her fingers were busy twisting a strand of hair that had somehow slipped loose from her pony tail.

"Yes you are," he said in a low voice never taking his eyes from hers. Her eyes were green and sparkled with the lights from the disco ball up on the ceiling.

The thin young man was standing beside them now. "Are you ready to go home now Lauren?" He asked her softly.

"She's no longer your date." Robert said and he stared at the smaller man daring him to make the first move. The young man opened his mouth as if to say something but before he could get it out Robert took Lauren's hands a second time and led her across the room and out the front door.

"I am now your ride home," Robert told her with a flourish of enthusiasm. "Just wait until you see my car!" He smiled that big confident grin, "I only travel first class!"

From this night on they were an item. Whenever he had time, he would spend it with her. His degree and his work were very important to him and he made it clear to her that she needed to understand that.

He lavished her with flowers and gifts when he did not have time for her and this kept her from feeling neglected. He became very good at flattering her. In fact he always knew just what to say and just what to do to keep her waiting.

"Robert, how are you doing?" she asked.

Finally, Maria had returned to unhook his IV's. She put a blue band-aid over the needle prick on his hand. He was free to catch a cab ride home and he felt so good he decided that he would surely be able to handle the side effects of the chemo.

No problem.

Chapter Four
Week Two of Chemo

Throughout the rest of the week he was relieved and excited to see that the chemotherapy seemed to have very little effect on him. Doctor Kimball did say that chemo was an accumulative effect. As each week goes by and the concentration in his body increases he may feel more side effects. He was so strong and in such good physical shape he was confident in beating it.

He worked hard the rest of the week to make up for the lost day. He was awarded a huge contract and went out to eat with a male co-worker to celebrate. He found out in the restaurant lounge, as they waited for their table, that he now had a new game to play with the ladies. When they found out he had cancer, they all felt the need to comfort him. He received long warm hugs and lots of attention. Several said, "If you ever need anything, just let me know."

Don't worry…he would.

Monday morning arrived again. He stood in the entryway outside of his house until he saw his cab cruising up the street to pick him up.

"To Southwest Hospital please," He told the cab driver. The drive to the hospital seemed long this morning. The traffic was heavy and there was an accident that they had to navigate around. Finally he was dropped off at the stone entryway and made his way into the building. He looked around as he checked in at the front desk and he finally saw his blue eyed angel. Maria was escorting an elderly woman from the waiting room. She smiled and gave him a quick wave.

"I'll be there in a moment." She said, "Have a seat."

Robert obediently sat down to wait. He could see her patting the woman's hand, trying to comfort her as they plodded slowly down the hall. He wondered if the elderly woman was a personal friend from the attention she was getting.

He looked around the crowded waiting room with it's sea of blue and brown flowered chairs.

He did not belong here. Any one could see he was totally out of place. These people looked tired and weak. Some wore scarves because they had lost their hair and only had peach fuzz patches covering their scalps. Some wore hats of many different kinds from baseball caps to stocking caps. Some had eyes that were sunk deep into their skulls with dark brown circles underneath. Though they all had one thing in common, they all looked defeated and very sad.

A car magazine caught Robert's attention on the coffee table. Wow! What a gorgeous car! He eagerly opened the magazine and the next thing he knew, Maria was standing in front of him asking, "Are you ready to go?"

"Sure," he said. "I was just checking out the new rides," and he pointed to the car on the front. "I'd look good in something like that."

"Let's get you through this chemo process first," she laughed. "Let's go back and get started."

Maria drew a vial of blood then left the room to deliver it to the lab. He hated having to wait for the results from Dr. Kimball. He looked over at the silver haired woman sitting across from him and realized she was sound asleep. Pitiful.

Finally his nurse came walking back in with her hand behind her back.

"I thought this might help pass your time," and Maria presented the car magazine to him. "A positive attitude is very important for your treatment," she smiled. "Just close your eyes and imagine getting well and treating yourself to that new car. That, in itself could be enough reason to keep you focused and to keep you looking forward to your future."

Robert started his new job in May of 1977, as soon as he graduated.
One of the first things he did was lease a Mercedes. He leased it because he wanted to change vehicles every year so it would always be the latest model and have the latest gadgets. Leather seating and a great stereo system were considered bare basics to him.
It was all about image.

He looked so forward to his future with this company and had expectations of much success. He was excited to get started.

Robert easily and quickly learned all of the features of his new product line and he was loaded with confidence when it came to cold calls on customers. He had no time to be intimidated by sales managers or company representatives.

His persistence paid off and he started to rack up impressive numbers right away. He caught the attention of his regional manager and he was offered a larger, more profitable territory after only eight weeks of work.

The new territory meant a transfer to Chicago, which was a town Robert hungered for due to the active nightlife and affluent neighborhoods. But it was a long distance away from Lauren.

He decided Lauren was very easy going and would not hold him back. She looked good on his arm and she always supported his ideas. His success depended on his ability to control his situations and as always, Robert had a plan.

"Marry me?" he asked he when he was saying goodnight to her at her dorm. "You don't need to go to school. I'll take

care of you." He never planned on letting her work after they were married anyhow, so why spend her parent's money.

"But I want to be a fashion designer!" Lauren said surprised. "I almost have one year done!"

"You don't know if you could make a lot of money as a designer. But I know I will, "he said softly, looking deep into her green eyes. "Let me take care of you." He held his arms out. "I love you, Lauren."

She flew into his arms and said "Yes!!" she hugged him tight. "Yes! I will marry you!"

"Thank you." Robert said satisfied. He had discovered that his regional manager hesitated to promote young single salesmen. The manager felt his salesmen were more motivated if they had a family to support and they were more stable. When Robert heard this he made sure the word got back to his supervisor that he was getting married and that was how he got the promotion.

Unfortunately, he did this <u>before</u> he asked Lauren to marry him. Obviously, he was a great catch. He knew she would say yes.

The next day Lauren was on a plane to Las Vegas. She wasn't even given the chance to tell her parents yet.

"Are you an adult or a child?" he had taunted her. "Do you need your Mommy's permission or can you think for yourself?"

As always, Lauren backed down to him. But if she was going to marry him, he was right. Why go through all of the expense and hassle of a ceremony? Though, she had always imagined holding her father's arm tightly as he walked her down the aisle. She had always imagined designing her own gown and arranging her own flowers. She quickly put that thought out of her mind to concentrate on the present.

After all, her new husband said, "Trust me. I will take care of everything." And she trusted him.

Their wedding ceremony was quick and to the point. Lauren carried a big bouquet of lilies which were only "rented" so she had to return them afterwards. She wore the rust colored dress she had worn the night they met. At least it was still a dress she had designed.

The official conducting the ceremony kept calling Lauren, 'Laura'. Even their marriage license referred to her as Laura

Jones. She pointed it out to Robert and asked to have it changed before they left the chapel. He said misspelling her first name wasn't important. As long as his name was spelled correctly it didn't matter because she would now be known as Mrs. Robert Jones.

Chapter Five
Chemo-Week Number Five

This week Robert was exhausted all of the time. He fell asleep in his desk chair one night and didn't wake up until the next morning. He had a terrible headache each evening and it didn't have anything to do with drinking Crown Royal.

The top of his hand was bruised and sore. It seemed he wore a band-aid on his the majority of the week. He had to, the scab would get bumped and bleed, always at the most inconvenient time.

One day it started to bleed while he was driving his Mercedes to a new account. He ended up getting blood on his leather seats and on the pale gray carpeting. He quickly pulled through a fast food drive through and asked for some napkins. The girl in the window handed them to him and was confused until she saw the blood. Then she handed him a stack of them. He had to have his car professionally cleaned afterward. It would have been too embarrassing to have a Mercedes with stained carpet.

On Friday night, his co-workers called him and asked him to go out drinking for their regular Friday night of partying.

"Hey! Robert!" Jake said. "We are meeting at Dilly's tonight. How does six o'clock work for you?"

"It's not going to work for me this time." Robert said with honest regret in his voice. "I think I've come down with a case of the flu." He paused, thinking of how to finish his lie. "I think I had better get myself some rest or I won't be able to whoop you guys in sales next week."

"You 'whoop' us in sales every week, rest or no rest." Jake laughed. "Sorry you will miss out tonight. We will keep track of all of the women we meet and we'll tell you all about it on Monday. Maybe we'll have better luck hunting females if you're not around!"

The truth was he was just too proud to say he couldn't drink because of his chemotherapy. He hated to give up his favorite weekend activity. But he knew he would have to fess up sooner or later.

Even worse than missing out on carousing with his friends was the fact that he noticed his food either tasted bitter or didn't have much flavor at all. Even his favorite spicy hot wings seemed bland, followed by his stomach grumbling and gurgling the rest of the night.

When he got out of the cab at the hospital he dreaded going in to start the chemo. The only thing that kept him going was being cared for by Maria.

As he walked from the parking lot on to the sidewalk he passed by the large plate glass windows and caught a glimpse of his reflection. His hair looked wind blown and he instinctively got his comb out and started to style it. As he went to put his comb back in his pocket he saw the clump of dark hairs dangling from it. He stopped dead in his tracks. It was happening. His hair was falling out. He carefully wound the long hairs around his middle finger and then pulled the coil off. He quickly stored the small roll of hair deep in the bottom of his trouser pocket. Somehow he couldn't bear to part with it at this time.

Maria was there to greet him. She led him straight back to the treatment room and she carried the conversation the whole way.

Robert sat in the straight backed chair quietly as she started taking the blood samples. He didn't even flinch this time when she inserted the needle.

"You're starting to have additional side effects, aren't you?" she asked softly.

"Yes," he said in a whisper. "How did you know?" He looked up to search her face.

"I've been doing this job for eight years." she said. "I figured it's been five weeks so it was about time since your chemo is so strong. I also noticed a change in your personality. It happens to everyone sooner or later."

"Well, I didn't think it would happen to me," he said. "I *always* win, but today I realize I may not have any control over this. I have to admit that it may be stronger than I am." He looked down at his arm, "And that scares me."

"Remember, Doctor Kimball is handling your case personally and all of your test results go directly to him." Maria patted him on the back. "He's a great doctor so that's a huge advantage. You're going to do just fine." She gave him a wink and headed out the door to take his blood sample to the lab.

The familiar silver haired woman was sitting slumped over in her chair across the room receiving her chemo. Her eyes were closed tightly and he noticed she seemed a lot thinner. He had seen Maria give her a hug as she walked by. She defiantly had something going for her because Maria seemed quite attached to her.

Robert sat there and looked at the four white walls surrounding him. Why is everything in a hospital so stark looking? Are colored walls less sterile than white ones? He doubted it. He figures it's somebody's idea of "looking clean and antiseptic."

He couldn't stand to look at the old lady any longer so he closed his eyes too.

Chapter Six
December 1977

Robert and Lauren moved into a high rise apartment in an affluent suburb of Chicago. It was close to the trains and all of the shops and night life but it was small and cramped. All of the walls of the apartment were solid white, which Robert disliked. Their landlords wouldn't allow them to paint any of the rooms to change the color. Robert hated the fact that they paid rent, BIG rent, but had no control over their surroundings.

Lauren seemed happy and content but she didn't look at things like he did. He was frustrated that he was one of the leading salesmen at a Fortune 500 company and some bozo that probably didn't even have a degree could tell him he had to live with white walls. Well, he'd fix the problem.

Robert walked in the door of the apartment one night after work.

"Lauren!" He called. "I have big news!" He went into the kitchen to try to find her. "Lauren, where are you?"

"Here I am," she said coming out of the laundry room with a stack of fluffy light blue towels. "What's the big news?"

"I bought us a house!" He announced triumphantly. "It's huge and we can paint the walls and decorate it any way we want to."

"You bought a house?" Lauren looked confused then disappointed "You bought a house without me?"

Robert stopped and threw his hands up in the air. "I have worked so hard to provide for my wife. I buy her a house, a _beautiful_ house, and it's just not good enough!" He paced back and forth raising his voice louder and louder as he continued.

"Nothing's ever good enough for my wife. I work and work and all she does is complain." He ranted and raved and then he grabbed his tan trench coat off of the back of the chair and headed for the front door.

"Start packing. It's a great house and you _will_ love it!" He slammed the door behind him for emphasis.

She knew he was going to Dilly's, the neighborhood bar. It seemed like a nightly routine for him to blow up and go get drunk. He said that it was her fault that he drank so much, since she never appreciated the things *he did for her. Maybe, she thought, if they could finally get out of this cramped apartment it would finally make him happy.*

Lauren was growing tired of his act. She was afraid to admit it but she thought she could smell perfume on him when he came home. She was tired of being alone all of the time. He would not allow her to have a car so she just existed in the small apartment every day.

She also missed her parents and longed to see them. She was delighted when he said they could spend Christmas with them. She was very excited to travel back home and celebrate the holidays together. At the last minute, Robert had an opportunity at a large commission, so he cancelled all of their travel arrangements.

Again, Lauren had to call her parents and make excuses on why they would not be home for Christmas. In the end, she spent the holiday alone and Robert spent it at the bar, coming home late in the evening smelling of Crown Royal and Coke.

After that she regretted not spending more time with her parents. In January, she got a call late one night. A deep voiced highway patrolman informed her that both of

Her parents had been tragically killed in a car accident earlier that evening.

They were T-boned by a drunk driver who had lost his license but still decided he could drink and drive. The funeral was more emotion than she could handle. Being an only child made it even more difficult.

She wished they were alive now because she knew they would have helped her figure out what to do and would have been happy to have her visit them or move in with them if she needed.

Chapter Seven
Chemo-Week Number Seven

Maria noticed how thin his hair was as she hooked up the tubes to the needle. She started the drip line so the process could begin.
"I received some new directions from Doctor Kimball. We are going to be increasing the concentration of the chemotherapy by another two percentage points. . Your Doctor did not feel you have made enough progress so we will try to speed it up." She gave him a squeeze on the shoulder. "You may have additional side effects in the next couple of weeks. But sometimes this means you can quit the chemo sessions a few weeks sooner."
"What kind of side effects are you talking about?" He asked, "I'm already so tired I don't think it's possible for that to get any worse."
"Well," she hated this part. It was not routine to increase the dosage to this level. She knew he would definitely notice the

difference and would probably be very miserable. But she was trained to always stay positive and only sat encouraging things.

"It varies from person to person. But you are strong so maybe it won't affect you very much." She gave him a quick one armed hug, "I will keep my fingers crossed for you. Let me know if you have additional side effects when you come next week."

Chapter Eight
March 1978

After the honeymooners moved into their new house, Lauren couldn't believe they were getting to live in such a wonderful big home in such an affluent neighborhood.

All of the houses had large lawns that were green and carefully manicured. The homes all had a minimum of three car garages and professionally installed landscaping. Most were equipped with alarm systems and motion detecting lights.

Their home had a huge stone entryway with columns across the front. As you walk in through the crystal glass double doors the marble floors lead to plush beige carpeting, Cherry cabinets and white crown molding accented all of the rooms.

There was a bedroom and a master bath off of the living room. The kitchen was spacious and had very expensive countertops and a professional gas stove fit for a chef. All of the appliances were harvest gold, which was the latest style, and they were all top of the line.

Just off of the kitchen, through a wood trimmed archway, was a dining room with a large crystal seven tiered chandelier. Their old dining room table was still in great condition but it looked very small in the large space. Lauren put in all of its leaves to make it as long as possible even though they had never had anyone join them for supper. It was always just the two of them.

Lauren was busy decorating and reorganizing the kitchen. Robert purchased all new pans for her. She was trying to decide which cupboards should hold which items. She had so many cherry wood cupboards to choose from, some ended up with only a serving dish or two in them.

A package came in the mail and was brought to the door by the postman. Since Robert did not like her to leave the house to shop she ordered some fabric from an ad in the newspaper. She was so excited to design and sew again. It had always been her passion.

She was making curtains for the two large kitchen windows. The fabric was white with small red rose buds scattered all over in a random pattern. She ordered matching white lace with a rose woven into the ruffled scalloped edging. She thought it was very beautiful. Robert was out of town all week so she had plenty of time to sew.

She cut and pinned and measured. It took her all day to create the rows of ruffles and the tightly hand sewn hem. It was three o'clock in the afternoon before she realized she hadn't even taken time to eat lunch.

A hot steam iron made the edges of the fabric crisp and professional looking. She slipped them onto the curtain rods late that night and sat back with a hot cup of cocoa admiring them. She so missed making things with her hands. It was very gratifying work.

Lauren decided to make a big dinner on Friday evening to celebrate her new curtains and to celebrate Robert coming home for the weekend.

His favorite meal was roast beef cooked with little carrots and potatoes. She made her special garlic gravy, which he always said was his favorite. She called him at his office to see what time he'd be home so she could have it all hot and ready.

"Robert?" his secretary Sara asked. "He left at noon for an appointment. He told me he would not be back to the office today."

"Thank You." Lauren answered flatly. Well, at least she knew he was back in town. She would plan to have the supper ready at 6:00. Hopefully the time would work out so all of the dishes were still fresh and hot when he arrived home.

She set the dining room table with their blue china and the creamy lace tablecloth. Three steel blue candles graced the center of the table. That morning she ordered a bottle of mid-priced wine to be delivered from the store. It arrived that afternoon and was sitting in a gold ornate ice bucket for a special treat. Sitting beside it were two cut crystal goblets just waiting to be filled.

She was excited for him to see her curtains. She was hoping he would allow her to take some classes in fashion design so she could finish her education. Maybe if he saw her work he would consider it.

At 5:45 she lit the blue candles. The roast came out of the oven but she kept the lid on tightly to keep it warm. The plates waited beside the stove in anticipation. The steamed asparagus was done to perfection. Hopefully he'd be home soon.

The clock chimed the half hour and she realized it was already 6:30. It chimed again and it was 7:00. She put the roast back in the oven on low heat. It was starting

to fall apart since it was so tender. A lot of people like their roast done to that stage, unfortunately Robert was not one of them.
Though she knew there was nothing she could do to change it.

At 8:35 she heard the garage door opener start up. Lauren saw the bright headlights slide their way across the living room wall. A car door creaked open in the attached garage, then slammed shut. She hustled into the kitchen and put the roast on the platter. As she was carrying it out into the dining room the front door swung open.

"What is this?" He demanded with a scowl as he pointed to the elaborate table setting.

"We are celebrating you being home for the weekend! She said enthusiastically. "And I have something else to show you!" she said with excitement. "Please, come in the kitchen and see."

He followed her past the dining room table into the kitchen. She pointed at the curtains on the two large windows.

"I designed these and sewed them myself." She was obviously pleased with herself. Then she asked timidly, "Do you like them?"

Now that she was standing closer to him, she could smell the alcohol, probably his favorite Crown and Coke. Had she known he had been drinking she probably wouldn't have shown him the curtains until the next morning. She never knew how he would react to a surprise when he was drunk.

He turned heel and headed back out to the living room. She followed closely with the bowl of asparagus and tried to change the subject.

"I made you supper." She said softly. "It's all of your favorite dishes."

"I'm not hungry," he barked, and he sunk down onto the couch.

"Are you sure?" she asked. "It's roast beef, carrots, little potatoes and asparagus."

"I said no!" He yelled. "I already ate!"

He stood up and stomped back into the kitchen. When she walked in he was standing looking at the bottom hem of the curtains, examining her work. Then he reached up and with a violent motion he grabbed the top of the curtain and pulled it off of the window, curtain rod and all.

"Do you do this to make fun of me?" He demanded. "Don't I make enough money

for you to buy curtains?" He reached up and ripped the second curtain down snapping the rod in two.

"How dare you put up homemade curtains on MY windows as if we were poor people." He shook his head in disgust. "I work day in and day out and it is never good enough for you, is it?" He left the kitchen in a rage.

Lauren ran over and gathered up the fabric and rods from the floor. She had worked so hard to make sure every stitch was perfect. They were constructed so much better than most purchased curtains. She pulled out the trash can and then stopped. She ran her fingers across the carefully placed ruffles. She folded the curtains in half and stored them in the pantry for now. Later she would hide them in her closet.

He came back into the kitchen and she panicked. She decided to avoid any more conflict.

"Robert," she said carefully. "You are right," she nodded her head thoughtfully. "I will get a ride to the store and I will find some new curtains for the kitchen. Those were awful"

"Who are you getting a ride with?" he said threatening. "Is it with that neighbor, the dentist, that I've seen checking you out when you go out to get the mail?" Robert came closer and closer to her. "Is that who you want to ride with?"

"No!" she objected. "I was going to call Tracy, Jack's wife." Jack was one of Robert's co-workers. Tracy told her at the last Christmas party that they should go shopping together some day. And Lauren thought it would be fun.

"No!" Robert snarled. "Jack is no longer my friend. He beat me at the last sales contest and that prize money should have been mine!" He pounded his fist on the table to show he meant it. "You will not socialize with someone I dislike!"

And with that he pushed by her as he headed for the kitchen door. She fell to the floor backwards and hit her head on the rung of the kitchen chair. She laid there dazed for a moment reeling from her injury. She heard the front door slam and she jerked from the noise. As she laid there with her head underneath the kitchen chair, she realized that he didn't even know she had fallen. Her eyes rolled back in her head and she passed out.

When she came to, she instinctively stayed perfectly still while she listened for any sound until she was sure she was alone. She sat up and felt the back of her head with her hand. It was throbbing and she found a large lump had developed right in the center.

She struggled to her feet, grasping onto the seat of the kitchen chair to get leverage. Her legs felt wobbly and her steps were shaky as she headed into the dining room.

His plate was used. As she laid in the kitchen unconscious, he must have come home from the bar hungry so he feasted on roast beef and vegetables. He left everything on the table where he found it and headed off to bed. He probably didn't even notice she was missing.

She slowly cleaned off the dining room table feeling weak and queasy the entire time. She put the leftovers into the refrigerator. She put the blue china dishes into the dish washer with the silverware and water glasses. She decided to sleep on the floor of the master bathroom.

She listened at the bedroom door for his snoring. It was loud and his breathing was slow and even so she knew he was asleep. She carefully tiptoed through to the bathroom and closed the door quietly behind her. Robert never even stirred.

Robert used the guest bathroom to get ready so she wouldn't be in his way in the morning. Having the bathroom door locked finally made her feel safe. She rolled up in her robe to keep warm while lying on the cold tile floor. A folded bath towel served as a pillow.

She decided not to brush her teeth or wash her face. The last thing she wanted to do was risk waking him up.

Chapter Nine
March 1978

At 5:00 yesterday, Robert had gone back to his office. He purchased a bouquet of white daisies, tinted with bright pink, for his secretary, Sara.

He held them behind his back as he entered the reception area, then revealed them to her.

"Sara, you work so hard every day," He said, "Would you have dinner with me tonight so I can pay you back for all of your work?" She looked at him questioning as he continued. "You are so valuable to me. I want to discuss the possibility of giving you a raise."

It was a good excuse to get her to go out with him. He really only wanted to explore to see if she was interested in him as more than a boss. He was pretty sure she was, and he decided he would be interested too.

After he added in the part about the raise she decided to go. Extra money would really help her out.

Sara told him that Lauren had called earlier that afternoon looking for him. Robert said his wife never listened to him. He clearly told her that he had plans tonight. She just didn't understand how demanding his job was. Besides she was never there for him. He made it clear that he was the victim in this marriage.

Sara wondered how he could have told Lauren he had plans this morning when he only asked her to have dinner ten minutes ago. She decided she wouldn't bring it up. It could definitely hurt her chances for the raise he was promising.

Robert carefully played the game. He complimented her choice of dress and how he could tell she'd been working out. When he talked to her he looked deep into her hazel eyes as if no one else existed. That was a trick that rarely missed. They enjoyed good conversation as they sipped their cocktails. He asked her many questions because he knew that women love to talk about themselves. They even discussed some gossip surrounding some of the other salesmen.

As they were finishing their salads he decided everything was looking positive, so he went for broke and suggested they stop at a motel that was on the way to her house, before he took her home.

She stared at him stunned for a moment. She pushed her chair back, and when she stood up she did so abruptly and she bumped the table and spilled water from their glasses.

"If that's what this is all about, then I quit!!" She threw her napkin down on the table. "Good luck finding another secretary that will put up with your harassment!"

She grabbed her black vinyl coat and headed to the door without putting it on. She looked over her shoulder and paused with one more furious stare, turned and was gone.

Just then the waitress came to their table with a tray full with their meals. Her eyes were wide since she witnessed the secretary's exit from the restaurant.

"Obviously," Robert said to the shaken waitress. "I will not want those meals. I will NOT eat alone."

"But your food, sir?" she stammered. "Sir? Your bill?" She was still holding the tray high in the air, unsure what to do with it.

"I'm not eating," he said gruffly. "So I'm NOT paying!!" He got up and grabbed his jacket off of the back of his chair and put *it on.* He tried to zip the front of his jacket but could not get the zipper started.

Frustrated, he marched away then stopped. He turned on his heel and stormed back to the table. He picked up his high ball glass still full of Crown Royal and Coke, took a drink and decided to take it with him.

"If you don't like it," he called over his shoulder, "Sue me!"

It didn't matter what Lauren would have said or done when he walked in the door and saw she had supper ready. He was so angry that Sara rejected him he was ready to lash out at anyone.

Chapter Ten
Chemo-Week Number Eleven

Robert found himself back at the treatment center of the hospital. He was careful to avoid the large plate glass windows. They were too reflective, and frankly he didn't want to see.

The weeks went by so quickly. He was so tired most of the time that he could barely function. His hair was quite thin by now and he had lost a lot of weight.

His job had always been his crowning glory of success. Now he could barely drag himself there each day and he found it very difficult to concentrate when he was with a client. He asked his boss if he could start coming in one hour later in the mornings. His boss said no. He said his job needed to be done during regular business hours, no exceptions. If he wanted to keep his job, he needed to work the long days.

Maria was working with the silver haired woman. She finally got her settled with a home decorating magazine and started her drip line.

"You work way too hard, Maria my dear." The silver haired woman said weakly as she watched her hustle from room to room and from patient to patient. "I think you could use some help."

"One of our nurses quit, so we're short-handed." Maria said. "They keep telling me they are trying to get someone hired but some days I have a mind to quit too. But of course I probably won't because I know I would miss all of you wonderful patients too much!" She smiled and scurried out of the door.

Robert closed his eyes and felt confident that last comment was directed at him. He hoped they would hire another RN so she wouldn't be stretched so thin.

Robert knew how hard it was to find good employees and frankly he had made many mistakes when it came to handling subordinates. He hated to admit it but he even regretted a few of his decisions.

Besides, he wasn't sure he could handle these chemo treatments without her.

Chapter Eleven
March 1978

When Lauren woke up the next morning she was stiff from sleeping on the cold tile floor. She reached up to smooth her hair and realized it was stiff with dried blood. She sat on the edge of the tub and finally the tears came. They started slowly at first and they turned into huge uncontrollable sobs. The mirror reflected huge swollen eyes. What did she do to deserve this life?

She did not know what time it was or if he was still in the house. She stood at the bathroom door holding her breath since all she could hear was the rise and fall of her chest. It was totally quiet so she slowly unlocked the door.

She peeked through the crack created by the open bathroom door for signs of Robert. He was not in the bed so she ventured out further to the bedroom door. As she listened at the hallway for any activity, her stomach started to reel. She walked out into the living room and looked in the garage to find Robert's car was gone.

As soon as she knew it was safe she headed back to the bathroom and sat on the floor by the toilet. Being sick to her stomach had to be from the injury Robert gave her last night. Before the thought was out of her mind the convulsions began. Every time she thought it was over, the cramps started up again. Finally she crawled on her hands and knees to the bed. She closed her eyes and dozed in and out for more than an hour.

When she woke up her stomach was growling loudly. She realized that she had not had any supper the night before. A roast beef sandwich sounded so good.

When she got into the kitchen she saw the bare windows. She rescued the curtains from out of the pantry and took them into the bedroom closet. She folded them carefully and put them in a box marked 'shoes.'

Someday she'd have a place to display them, until then she'd keep them safe in her closet.

Chapter Twelve
March 1978

Robert looked around the fitness club. He ate way too much, way to late last night. As soon as he got up this morning he knew he needed to get to the gym.

Robert did the treadmill for an hour until he had worked up a huge sweat, then he started on the stair climber.

What had he been thinking? Not only did his night fall apart, he now would have to hire and train a new secretary. His last secretary, Sara, had been exceptional at her job. She always seemed to be one step ahead of him and he would miss that. The more he thought about her good work, the more he regretted asking her to share a motel room. Maybe if he apologized, he could get her back.

He decided he would go over to her apartment as soon as he was done with his exercise routine. He was really good at fake apologizing, and the real crazy thing was, this time he would really mean it.

It worked, though it cost him a raise of $75.00 per week to get her back. He decided it was worth it. He had to apologize over and over and he had to go on and on about how he couldn't make it without her. He begged her to give him a second chance and finally she said yes.

They would start out fresh on Monday morning and he guaranteed her that it would be strictly professional.

It was early evening when he arrived home. He walked in the door and dumped his brief case by the chair. He kicked off his designer alligator shoes to reveal a hole in the big toe of his sock. He pulled his socks off and went into the kitchen to throw them into the trash.

The savory smell of beef stew made him realize he hadn't eaten all day. Lauren was sitting at the table and quickly said as she got up, "I'll have the table set and ready for you in five minutes."

Robert pulled out a dining room chair and waited. He enjoyed being waited on and anyhow he still had a hangover. How could Crown and Coke be so fun on one hand, but so miserable on the other hand.

The bowl of stew Lauren put in front of him looked good and tasted even better. She was a pretty good cook. Of that he could not complain.

Lauren sat down in front of a bowl of steaming hot stew to join him. He obviously had no idea he had knocked her out the night before. She hated to start a conflict with him when things were going so well, so she decided not to say anything. He would just tell her it was her fault anyhow.

The beef stew looked good. The veggies were simmered just right, tender but not overcooked. The chunks of roast were seasoned perfectly and juicy on the inside.

Suddenly the smell was churning Lauren's stomach. After only a few bites she pushed back her chair and ran to the bathroom. He could hear her vomiting even though the door was tightly closed.

"What's her problem," he wondered. "Oh well, she'll get over it." He made the mental note to keep his distance. He couldn't afford to catch a virus from her and get sick right now, he was entirely too busy.

He enjoyed his stew so much he got up and served himself another bowlful.

Chapter Thirteen
Chemo-Week Fifteen

Robert was so tired after his chemo this week he did not make it to work that afternoon or the next day. He forgot he had scheduled a meeting with a client and was called in to the District Managers office.

"I'm sorry to be the one to do this, considering what you are going through, but you forgot your meeting with Mr. Swenson from Pro Industries, yesterday." The District Manager continued avoiding eye contact with Robert.

"Mr. Swenson is so upset that he said there will not be any future orders and he's refusing to take delivery on his existing orders. Our company is going to feel the loss of this client for a very long time. Because of this we are letting you go effective immediately." Finally, he looked Robert directly in the eye for emphasis.

"I have worked here for almost twenty years!!" Robert said in disbelief. "I can't believe you are firing me over one missed meeting!! Do you realize I have major bills and I have to have a job to survive!!" He begged, "Plus I have cancer!!"

"It has always been our policy to fire anyone that costs this company a major account. And this *was* a major account. Again I am sorry, but you have one hour in which to gather your things and I will need to accompany you out of the building." He said with a note of finality.

Robert stood up and stormed from the room. "You haven't heard the last from me!!" He yelled back at the District Manager. He went to his office, dumped everything personal from his desk into his trash can and used it to carry his belongings to his car.

The District Manager stood by quietly, and Robert bit his tongue. He would let his lawyer do his talking tomorrow. He was afraid if he said what he was thinking right now he would surely say things he would regret.

Chapter Fourteen
Chemo-Week Number Sixteen

"Are you ready for your treatment?" Maria asked as she patted him on his back softly.

She was the saving grace in all of this. She hadn't even mentioned the fact he had lost the majority of his hair and his eyebrows were getting very sparse. He had no idea he would look so different without his dark brows.

"Yes," He replied. "Do I have a choice?"

"You do," she paused. "But the alternative is not much fun." She stuck the needle in to draw a blood sample and could not get any blood. She stuck him a second time again with no luck. His hand had so many purplish red prick marks it reminded her of someone with a drug problem.

"We will need to start using the inside of your elbow from now on. This vein is full of scar tissue and needs a rest."

She leaned over and started rolling up

his sleeve. Robert decided it was worth all of the pain and discomfort just to smell her floral perfume.

Since his appearance started to change women were a little tough to come by. They were nice enough, but instead of chasing after him, they felt sorry for him. It worked for a while when he still looked healthy, but now he felt they treated him like he had the plague or something and they were afraid to get too close so they wouldn't catch it.

"As soon as you are done with these treatments," Maria said. "Your hair will grow back in and he would be strong again. That day couldn't come too soon for him."

Maria purposely left out the part where his hair may not be as thick or be the same texture as it was before. Some patients come in with thick wavy hair and find it grows back in super curly or thin and flat. Since there was a chance it could grow back in like it was before, she decided to keep that info to herself. As always, she maintained her positive attitude.

He also noticed a huge change in his professional life since being fired. He was sure another chemical company would be thrilled to hire him as quick as possible. He called several competitors but got the same song and dance about 'times being tough' and they 'would call him if they got an opening'.

His normal confidence was waning and with his increased chemo concentrations he was absolutely miserable.

Everyone could see something was wrong yet felt the need to ask him, "Are you okay?" To which he would reply that he would be if they would help him out by giving him a job.

He still was very proud and didn't want their pity. He emphasized to everyone that he would work his butt off to make them glad they hired him. But everyone had an excuse.

The truth of his situation was he had never been good at saving money and when he saw something he liked he had to have it. Along the way he maxed out several credit cards, always sure he could earn the money as time went by to keep up with his payments. He was earning unemployment, but it did not even cover his house and his Mercedes payments. In a few days, the reality set in that he would need to change his life style in order to avoid bankruptcy.

Maria returned from the lab saying his blood samples had high enough white blood cell counts so they could start the chemo therapy now. She dragged the metal IV stand towards him with a familiar screech.

"Oh goody," was his monotone reply. "I can't wait!" He said sarcastically. He closed his eyes as she inserted the clear plastic tubing onto the needle. He waited for the cold numb feeling he always got as the IV bag started to empty its contents into his blood stream.

The elderly lady that was scheduled to share his appointments each week finally walked in. She excitedly told Maria about her new granddaughter, Ava, born the night before. Maria looked thrilled to hear the news. Maybe they had a connection outside of the hospital. Maria always treated them both so special and she seemed so excited about the birth. He closed his eyes and listened to the grey haired woman talk on and on about her new grandbaby in every detail.

There was only one baby in Robert's life, and that was long ago.

Chapter Fifteen
April 1978

"Mrs. Jones?" the doctor said. "It is Mrs. Jones?" she nodded 'yes' and he continued. "I have wonderful news for you!" He smiled broadly, "You are eleven weeks pregnant."

Lauren could not believe what she was hearing! She had just made plans to leave Robert and move in with a friend. Her friend barely had room for her yet alone a baby. Her friend agreed because she really could use another person to help pay the monthly rent.

How could she support a baby by herself? Who would hire a pregnant woman? How could she pay her fair share of the rent? The answer was she couldn't.

The heavy set doctor was talking in a low raspy voice about appointments, a prescription vitamin and what to expect from this process.

All Lauren could grasp from the conversation was she would have to stay living with Robert, at least until the baby was born.

Lauren did not tell Robert she was pregnant for four weeks. Every time she thought she would tell him he would come home late, smelling of alcohol, or upset about some deal that fell through.

They had discussed having children early in their marriage and it had been a disappointing discussion.

"Do you think I'm made of money?" Robert had argued. "I've worked hard for what we have, I'm not sure I want to share." He concluded, "Children are very expensive and I am NOT ready."

Finally she could wait no longer. She could hide the morning sickness and the constant cravings from him, but not the fact that her stomach was stretching quickly and soon she would need new clothes.

"A baby?" Robert asked. "Are you sure?" He looked at Lauren closely. Was this a trick? Was she telling the truth?

"Yes, I'm sure." Lauren said quietly. She held her breath, afraid for Robert's reaction because she really had no idea how he would respond.

"I went to the doctor this week," She looked down as she spoke. "They did blood and urine tests and they came out positive."

She cautiously looked him in the eye to try to read what he was thinking. "I was surprised too."

"This is wonderful!!" Robert said with enthusiasm. After all, he had seen salesmen with families getting promoted at his job and he could only imagine what having a child would mean for his position.

"I'm so glad you're happy about it!" Lauren said still not sure if he could be believed. Her level of trust when it came to him was almost zero. If he was telling the truth though, this could make her situation of needing to stay with him a little easier.

The next few months went along with little conflict. Robert knew that Lauren was often bored in the past. The baby seemed to give her something to look forward to and being pregnant seemed to make her happy. Plus he didn't worry so much about her having an affair or leaving him. She now needed him for support and that is how he preferred it.

Robert didn't understand why every one made such a big deal about pregnant women. He really found their enlarging abdomen's to be grotesque. Their faces broke out with acne, their feet were swollen and they were tired all of the time. What was so great about all of that? What was in it for him?

Lauren was happy for the first time in a long time. She nearly dismissed the lump she had received on the back of her head. She grew more positive that he had no idea that she had been hurt.

Plus, being pregnant was like having a secret little friend with you at all times. She did not feel alone or lonely any longer.

The first kicks were amazing. At first she thought she had a muscle spasm but when the little flutter feeling kept reoccurring she realized what it was.

Since Robert was so busy at his work he allowed Lauren to get a cab ride to her doctor's appointments. She enjoyed getting out of the house even if for a short while.
He often called at the time he expected her home though to make sure she wasn't making any additional stops.

She was finally past the morning sickness stage and she was very grateful to have that over with. Now she had indigestion, where if she ate anything that was spicy or strongly flavored she tasted it over and over.

She also felt the need to sit real straight and tall to relieve the pressure on the bottom of her rib cage. Some days she stretched way back over the back of the chair she was sitting in to relieve the aches and pains.

At each doctor's appointment the doctor checked her over and she always checked out healthy. The months went by very quickly.

"The baby is doing just fine!" he reassured her. "Just keep eating healthy foods and watch your caffeine intake."

The Doctor put his hand on hers and said, "You're doing great!"

Robert was gone a lot on business trips. Lauren was glad he was gone. She had evidence every time he came home that he was having affairs. One week, there was lipstick on the lapel of his jacket. Another week his handkerchief smelled strongly of perfume. Lauren didn't really care since she planned on leaving as soon as the baby was born. She didn't think Robert would be able to handle a crying infant and she would not risk her baby to his anger.

Whenever he came home drunk she stayed as far out of his way as possible. Usually, she just said she was tired and headed off to bed early. Life settled into a dull routine, blissfully low on conflict.

Chapter Sixteen
August 1978

Robert decided to buy baby room furniture for the guest room of their house. He picked out a comforter set in pale yellow and a baby bed that had roses carved into the wooden headboard. It was the top of the line when it came to baby furniture. He decided to have it delivered as a surprise for Lauren.

The sales woman that helped him was named Sasha. She caught his eye as soon as he strolled into the store. He walked up to her and asked, "Could you help me? I'm here to spend money."

When he told her his wife was having a baby she led him to the infant furniture area. He told her that he had always wanted to be a "Daddy." He said he wasn't in love with his wife any longer but he was doing whatever he could to take good care of his child. He was aware that women melted from comments like that and Sasha was no exception.

He picked out the bed and bedding and she couldn't believe what a huge heart this guy had. He kept saying his baby needed the best. He saw how impressed she was and he decided they should have some new dining and living room furniture too.

"This living room set is the latest style," Sasha said. "But it is on the more expensive end. I haven't had very many customers able to afford it"

"Money is not an issue," Robert said bragging. "I only go first class!" He smiled knowing he had impressed her, and said," I'll take it all, and I want it delivered."

The next morning a truck pulled up into the driveway of their house. The driver, a short stocky man with a thick salt and pepper mustache, came to the door and said he had a truck load of new furniture for a 'Mrs. Robert Jones'.

Laura signed the delivery papers very confused. "I didn't order any furniture," she said though she had been looking forward to shopping for a few new pieces.

"Just a moment," she said. "I need to call my husband." She quickly called Robert to ask him about the delivery.

"You're welcome," he said sarcastically. "I didn't want you to have to go from store to store to find the pieces we needed, so I picked it all out for you." His surprise wasn't getting the reaction he expected. "I was just trying to make things easy for you. I thought you would appreciate it."

"I do appreciate it," she said backing down. "But I was looking forward to shopping with you for the furniture." She tried to hear a hint of understanding in his voice, but it wasn't there.

"I never do things good enough for you, do I." He said flatly. "I'll talk to you later." And he hung up the phone abruptly.

The delivery men were very helpful. They removed the crates from the couches and chairs, assembled legs and attached chair arms.

One of the men was tall and very slender. He appeared to be in charge of the crew. He happily helped her set the new furniture in its place and even carried an old overstuffed chair down into the basement for her.

They were so kind and went above and beyond what was necessary that she went into the bedroom and took some money out of her stash in her underwear drawer to give them as a tip. She also fixed them a container of fresh baked cookies for their trip home.

She had to admit that she really enjoyed the company. It had been a long time since she had new people to talk to.

After the men left she looked around the rooms of the house. The furniture was very formal with velvet fabrics with rose patterns woven in. The wooden arms and legs were carved with ornate decorations.
It was not very comfortable to sit on, it was nothing she would have picked out, but it did look terribly expensive. It would impress Robert's co-workers and clients. She was sure that was why he chose it.

Robert knew she wouldn't have wanted furniture like this for their everyday use. By surprising her with it, he had total control over the furniture that they bought.

She decided she shouldn't complain. Most wives would be very lucky to have furniture like this.

Robert's furniture purchase must have been worth a huge commission for Sasha because when he asked her to have a drink when she got off from work, she said yes.

He took her to the Hilltop, the most expensive bar in the downtown area. The corners of the bar were dimly lit and the booths were cozy. Robert walked in and asked to be seated in a quiet area so they could talk. He also preferred the shadowy areas because he never knew if he would run into a client or someone he knew. If the truth be known, the risk of getting caught just made the whole cheating thing more intoxicating to him.

"Mixed drink?" He asked Sasha. "Or are you more the champagne type?"

"Surprise me." She said knowing he'd pick the champagne. As he told her at the store, he "only goes first class."

"Bring me your best bottle of champagne," he requested, "and a Crown and Coke." He had eaten a good supper, surely that would prevent a hangover.

Robert started his routine. He looked her directly in the eyes as if she were the only person in the room. He also was very interested in everything she did. He found out she was an adult college student studying psychology. She had worked at the furniture store for the past eight years. She revealed that she was the top sales person at the furniture store and had been for the last three years. *Being in sales himself he was always interested in talking with someone that could sell successfully.*

"How come you are the top salesperson now, but you weren't for the first five years?" he asked. "What are you doing different," then he smiled mockingly. "Or was did the former top salesperson quit?"

Sasha took offense at that suggestion.

"No one quit, the past top salesperson is still there. They are just not the top anymore." Then she added, "I've become a personality expert. By knowing people's personality's and how they think I've been able to triple my sales."

"So you're saying that when each person walks into the store you try to figure out their personality so you will know how to make them buy stuff so you can increase your sales?" Robert asked interested.

"Yes," she admitted. "That's exactly what I do."

"So what's my personality?" he asked. "Oh! And by the way, I was going to buy all of that furniture either way. It had nothing to do with you selling it to me."

Sasha laughed out loud. "Ok, if that's what you want to believe." *The change of*

Robert's expression should have warned her to stop.

"You still haven't told me my personality type." He questioned persistently. "Or am I too complicated?"

"No, not at all," she said. Knowing his personality she should have backed off. But it was a crowded bar and it seemed pretty safe. "Your personality type is very easy to predict."

"I am not your ordinary person, so I doubt you can predict what I am thinking." He said challenging her.

"I know you have a narcissistic personality just like millions of other people." She said, knowing full well that he would not like the idea that he is similar to lots of other people. One attribute of this personality is they always feel superior and more successful than almost everyone.

Narcissists are also preoccupied with a sense of entitlement. They feel people should always take care of their needs first, and do things their way, no matter what. It's a control issue.

Another attribute is a lack of empathy. Robert told her that his wife was 34 weeks pregnant and that Lauren didn't understand how hard that made life for him. When she had morning sickness, he had to eat breakfast late quite often because she had to keep running to the bathroom to throw up. How was he supposed to work all day without his usual breakfast?

"I resent that!!" Robert said loudly placing both of his hands flat on the table in front of him.

"I am not arrogant. Can I help it if other people are continually jealous of me?" He continued, "This is a bunch of bull crap!"

"Well." She ventured. "I knew you would order champagne if I left it up to you. I also knew you would buy the most expensive furniture we had, not so much that you liked it, but because I told you it was very expensive and very few people could afford to buy it. You felt it would be a reflection on yourself and your success. All I had to do was massage your ego and you would buy whatever I showed you"

"Well!!" he said very defensive. "I don't have to sit here and listen to this. I have more important things to do." With that he got up and stomped out of the bar.

How dare she laugh at him! She had no idea just who she was talking to!

"*Besides, I don't have a problem, it's the rest of the world that has the problem!*"
Definitely a classic case of personality disorder. Sasha smiled and poured herself another glass of champagne. No reason to let it go to waste. She snuggled back into the heavily padded seat. She may as well relax and enjoy it.

When Robert got home from the bar he looked around the living room at the new furniture. It looked good, good and expensive. He actually liked how she arranged it.
He bought this furniture because he liked it, not because he cared what other people think or because of anything Sasha said. How dare she laugh at him! That's the last time he would go into that furniture store. They just lost a very good customer with plenty of money to spend.
"I like it," he said to himself and he slowly nodded his head in approval. Then his expression changed to a frown.
"Lauren!!" She was in the bath room and heard him yelling from the living room. "How did you get all of this furniture into

place?" He demanded. "You are eight months pregnant!"

"The delivery men were wonderful!" she exclaimed as she hurried out to meet him. "They helped me set it all up and hauled away the crates and trash." She smiled brightly hoping he would be pleased they had helped her.

"You liked that, did you?" He looked at her with piercing eyes. "What else did they do for you? How grateful were you for their help?" He asked as he walked toward her.

"I was grateful but not like you are suggesting!!" She laughed and patted her stomach. "You have got to be kidding!!" She argued back, "Anyway they were just doing their jobs."

"Don't argue with me and don't laugh at me!" Robert demanded. "Don't EVER laugh at me!" He got close and right in her face. "I'm sure they did their jobs real well, didn't they? DIDN'T THEY?"

She ducked under his arm and took off at a dead run back to the master bathroom. Before she could get the door shut behind her he pulled it back open. "Don't you run from me," he yelled. "Don't you EVER run from me!"

He grabbed her by the hair and pulled her backwards out of the bathroom. He grabbed her roughly by the shoulders and shook her, yelling the entire time. His face was so close to hers she could smell the liquor on his breath and it made her nauseous.

When he finally let go she stepped back and let months of pent up frustration take over. Without thinking she raised her hand and slapped him firmly across his cheek. The noise from the slap echoed through the room. Then it was totally silent for a few seconds.

"I'm so sorry," she stammered breaking the silence. "I'm so sorry. I didn't mean to"

"You bet you'll be sorry." he said gritting his teeth as he spoke. "Do you realize I could call the police right now and have you thrown into jail for assault?"

He felt the side of his face. It was now turning bright pink

Lauren took the opportunity to run. She moved as fast as possible back into the master bathroom. She quickly locked the door behind her. In the dark, she vowed that he couldn't treat her this way. She realized waiting until the baby was born was a mistake. She had to protect the baby no matter what. She would find a job and go back to school.

Maybe an old friend would let her stay on their couch until she could get their divorce finalized. She had no idea what their finances were like but there always seemed to be plenty of money to throw around. If she could get enough money to get by for awhile things would work out

She would try to leave as soon as he was gone. He had to go out of town this next week. That would give her a head start so he wouldn't be able to find her. If only she had a car and could drive. She'd be gone before he knew what happened.

"Open this door!" Robert demanded from outside in the bedroom. "Open this door, NOW!!" He was beating on the door with his fist. The door strained against the force of his fist with each blow.

"I'm going to call the police if you don't come to the door! I will! I will call the police." She sunk down in the bathtub and held her hands tightly against her ears to block out his yelling. She hoped he would go away, hoping the door would hold.

Finally, there was quiet. She heard his footsteps fade down the hallway. She curled up in the tub and laid there for what seemed like a very long time. The front of her blouse was soaked with tears and she shivered from the cold and from fear. She was thankful she could hide in the dark as she drifted off to sleep.

"Ma'am?" A voice asked waking her from her fitful sleep. "Mrs. Jones, are you okay?"

"Who are you?" She answered timidly. "Yes, I'm okay." She added, "Who are you?"

"I am Sergeant Wilson. Sergeant Larry Wilson." His voice was controlled and calm. "Could you open the door please?"

"Is my husband out there?" she asked. "I don't want to come out if he's there."

"It's okay," he answered. "He's in the kitchen with my partner being interviewed. You can come out so we can talk. I assure you, it's safe."

She stood up stiffly and stepped out of the tub. Her back was terribly stiff and she ached from head to toe.

"Are you sure it's okay?" She asked with her hand frozen on the door lock.

"It's okay," he reassured her. Just unlock the door so we can talk."

A loud metal click signaled the door was unlocked. She twisted the knob and opened the door revealing the face of the kind voice.

Sergeant Wilson was a tall man in his mid thirty's. His dark blue uniform was in sharp contrast to his short cropped blond hair and blue eyes. He smiled at her and said, "Thank you for opening the door. Come out here and talk with me." He stepped aside so she could pass through. "What is this all about?"

Suddenly she was racked with emotion. She started to sob and struggled to speak. "He was so mad at me!!" She started. "He was so terribly mad!"

"Why was he mad?" The officer inquired.

"He had furniture delivered here yesterday and he started to accuse me of being interested in the men who unloaded it." She put her hand on her bulging stomach. "I told him it was ridiculous to think the men would be interested in me since I'm thirty-four weeks pregnant." She started to cry again. "But he was drunk and just kept shaking me and yelling at me."

She looked down and admitted, "Then I slapped him to get him to stop. I didn't mean to, it just happened."

Sergeant Wilson listened carefully. He had been involved in many domestic abuse cases, in fact, far too many. He could see the fear in her eyes, and believed that there was reason for her to be afraid.

"Did he hurt you in any way? Do you have a visible injury?" She shook her head no. "Please sit here for a moment. I need to confer with my partner."

Sergeant Jeff Davis was seated in the kitchen talking with Robert. He was coming to talk to Sergeant Wilson and they met in the dining room where they could keep track of both parties involved. He was a heavy set man and he looked over at Lauren as they talked. His wife was also pregnant so he could relate to her condition.

"He's drunk and says she slapped him and there's a definite bruise on his cheek to collaborate his story. " He hated cases like this one. It was hard to know who was at fault.

"She admitted that she slapped him and I can't find any evidence that she was hurt," said Sergeant Wilson. They both knew what that meant. It was very cut and dried when it came to the laws in situations like this. They each headed back to their witnesses. Lauren was still seated on the couch in the living room.

"Mrs. Jones?" Sergeant Wilson said. "Could you please stand up?" Pregnant Lauren struggled to get to her feet. With a helping hand from the officer she finally was standing up in front of him.

"Turn around please," the officer requested. Lauren turned and was surprised when he took her hand and slipped a cold metal handcuff around her wrist.

"What?" She asked confused. "What are you doing?" Her voice rose to a higher pitch. "He threatened me! I'm sorry I slapped him. I know it was wrong, I know it! But he threatened me! I had to protect my baby!" He now had her right wrist and was cuffing it to the left one.

"Oh please! I didn't mean too!" she pleaded. "I didn't mean too!" she tried to see his face over her shoulder, but his expression was blank. He was just doing what the law required.

In a domestic abuse situation, someone had to go to jail. In this case the injury was visible on the husband so he had no choice but to take the wife in to be charged. He led her out of the living room and to the front door.

"Do you need any medications to go with you?" He asked.

"I only take maternity vitamins, but I don't need them until morning." She answered.

"Well, we need to get them then," he said. "You won't be released until sometime tomorrow, late morning at the soonest." He looked toward his partner. "Could you please get them?"

Robert jumped into the conversation. "I'll show you her bathroom. I want to make sure my baby has what it needs." And he led the officer toward the hallway.

As he rounded the corner to the hallway he looked back at Lauren. "At least one of us is concerned about the welfare of our baby."

Lauren followed the officer out of the front door. Several neighbors were standing in their driveways waiting to see what was happening. It wasn't often two police cars were in their neighborhood with their lights brightly flashing.

The neighbors often heard Robert yelling and were aware of a few heated arguments coming from this house but they *did not expect Lauren to be the one taken to jail.*

The officer opened the back door of the police car and asked Lauren to duck her head as she got in. Her face was streaked with tears. She was trembling so violently the officer asked, "Are you cold? Do you need a jacket?"

"No," she said. "I'm just scared." She looked up at him with huge eyes. "I've never been in trouble before. I'm so scared." And the tears started to flow again.

"It will be fine, just be honest and we can get this resolved." He reassured her.

"Make sure to tell us everything." He said, "It's very important that we have all of the details." He felt there was a whole lot more to this story than what she told him. In these cases, there almost always was.

After the police left, Robert was so tired all he could think of was sleep. He hated to call the police on her, but she gave him no choice. He could not let her get away with slapping him.

Again, Crown and Coke meant he would get a good night sleep. And he crawled into bed, sighed and fell into a sound sleep.

Chapter Seventeen
Chemo-Week Number Eighteen

It was morning again. He stood at the bathroom sink brushing his teeth. He tried to ignore the fact that most of his hair was missing. But now he examined his eyes and realized he only had a few eye lashes left. He decided he looked like he was 80 years old. His face was all wrinkled and dry. His sunken eyes had no color what so ever except for the huge dark circles beneath them. The gums of his teeth had started bleeding when he brushed them, even though he tried to be careful. Today was no different.

It was Monday, the day to have another treatment. Ever since Doctor Kimball increased the strength of the chemo concentration he had a lot more severe side effects. He spent the majority of his time sitting on the tile floor of his bathroom, emptying the contents of his stomach into the toilet. And when the contents were gone, dry heaves followed until his ribs were sore and bruised. This was no way to live, but it was also no way to die. He was trapped in this world of cramps and convulsions and saw no way out.

He thought about running away, and of abandoning his treatments, but he had invested so much time, money and pain in his cure, he felt determined to finish.

He had always been proud of his determination. Right now, it was all he had left. That, and getting to see Maria.

Her strength was so important to him. He was sure she had provided encouragement to many patients over the years, but he really believed that he was special and he was getting special treatment because she sincerely cared about him.

He had a lot to tell her this week. He decided to let his house go back to the bank. It was a terribly hard decision for him to make, and in the end he simply had no choice. It would be taken forcibly if he didn't give it.

He had loved everything about the house. The grand entry way that made him feel important every time he walked up the driveway, the rich tile floors and the harvest gold countertops that felt cool to his touch. To let it all go was a huge concession for him.

He had been so proud of being part of that neighborhood. He was surrounded by doctors, dentists and lawyers. Robert admired the prestige that came with their degrees. He enjoyed surrounding himself with people of importance. Even though he moved out last week he still drove by the house every night. Sometimes he parked by the curb across the street and just sat and looked at the house.

All of his new furniture had been repossessed by the credit card company and so his current residence in an apartment had very little furnishings. It was a depressing place to exist.

A lady in the waiting room asked him where he was from. He gave her his old address on Cherry Hill Lane. Even to an old feeble woman he couldn't admit his current situation, he was still so vain.

He knew no one was going to hire him in his current medical condition. And even if they did, he was so weak since his chemo was increased, he probably would not make very good commissions. If he did not make big money who would he be? His image was everything to him. He thought maybe Maria could give him some advice.

"Let it go," she said. "Your record of amazing performance will still be there after you have your strength back. There's a lucky company out there just hoping someone of your ability will walk in wanting a job. They'd be crazy not to want you!" She said. "Give yourself a break and less stress will probably help you get well faster."

If he was out of work for very long he would not only have lost his job and his house, he could also lose his car and his ability to buy the designer clothing he was so fond of. Unfortunately, he had maxed out his credit. Every time he bought something he put it on plastic. He was so far in debt that there was very little flexibility in lowering his need for money. He would be ruined.

"It's time!" Maria came back in with the bag of chemo to hang on the IV stand.

"Your white blood cells are still sufficient for you to receive another treatment." She started to insert the tube into the end of the needle. The familiar cold feeling quickly spread up his arm and through out his body.

He closed his eyes to sleep.

Chapter Eighteen
August 1978

Robert crawled out of bed the next morning. He went to the hallway bathroom to get ready. He was going to go to the fitness club to work out. Exercise was good therapy for him when he was frustrated, and right now he was very frustrated.

He regretted having Lauren arrested, but she had asked for it and it was for her own good so she could learn she could not treat him that way.

He was always trying to help her by showing her better ways to talk, better ways to wear her hair, how to dress herself and how to keep an organized house. He was always trying to help her to be the best she could be. But she rarely appreciated his help. It just proves how ignorant she is.

He was mad at Lauren for being so ungrateful for his gift of the furniture. How dare she question his taste! Nothing was ever good enough for her. That furniture cost thousands of dollars and he bought it because they deserved the best even though the payments would be a stretch. He would just need to continue working very hard. It would be well worth it.

It was Lauren's own fault that he needed to find comfort with other women. Most women would be thrilled to trade places with her. She didn't have to work outside if the home and he gave her everything she needed. But she still never seemed to be satisfied.

He went to the phone to call the police station to see when he could pick Lauren up. When he got there he noticed the answering machine alerted him he had a message by flashing its red light. He pushed the button to broadcast the message.

Chapter Nineteen

Lauren stared at the plain white ceiling from the hospital bed. Tears couldn't come any more, there were none left.

In the middle of the night, she had experienced pain across her lower back. She thought it was from the thin mattresses on the metal framed bunk bed she was forced to sleep on.

Suddenly she realized there was warm water all over the lower mattress. It was the baby. Her water had broken.

"Guard!" She yelled. "Help me!" Several other inmates woke up and joined her in yelling for the guard. Lauren finally heard the matronly woman come down the hallway with her keys jingling.

"Help me!" She begged. "I'm thirty-four weeks pregnant and I think my water just broke!"

The guard looked her over and then used her radio to call for help. About ten minutes later a gurney was bumping down the hallway, stopping in front of her cell, attended by first aid trained prison personnel. There were two men that were normally called to treat stomach aches and fist fight victims, not premature births.

The jail ambulance was called and they loaded her on board, strapping her down for the lengthy trip to the hospital. It would have taken too long to wait for the city ambulance since the city hospital was on the other side of the city.

Unfortunately, security does not allow for a prisoners quick release, even in emergency situations. By the time she was put into the ambulance, the pain across her stomach and back was excruciating.

"My body wants me to push!!" She said.

"You can't push!" the attendant said. "How many weeks along are you?"

"I'm thirty four weeks." She gasped out in total panic. "I still have six weeks to go!" The tears flowed again.

"Try to remain calm if at all possible." He explained. "Your baby has a chance if we can keep it from being born."

But it was too late. The small head had crowned and was making its way out of the birth canal. The attendant saw no choice but to help deliver the tiny body.

Layla fought hard to breath, but her lungs weren't developed at thirty four weeks.

The attendant kept apologizing. He kept saying they weren't equipped to handle a premature delivery.

They tried to give the baby oxygen but she was too tiny for their equipment. They allowed Lauren to hold Layla as they held the oxygen mask to her face, covering her nose and mouth. Layla looked up at Lauren with huge dark eyes. Lauren knew those few moments may have to last forever. She tried to memorize the tiny curve of Layla's head and the little up turned nose. She was covered with a white waxy substance which the attendant said was common for premature babies. Lauren didn't care. She was just glad she finally got to hold her secret little friend and got to look into those eyes.

"Layla," she said softly. "That's your name, I hope you like it." She continued, "I have loved you from the day I knew I was pregnant. And I will love you forever. I am so glad I got to hold you. It is so important that I got to look into your eyes. Be strong my baby, we're almost there!"

"Her pressure is dropping." The attendant said. "We are still about ten minutes from the hospital. She's not responding to the oxygen."

They took the tiny body from Lauren's arms. They laid her right beside Lauren's head and tried to fit the mask tighter across her face. Layla stared at Lauren the whole time with those huge dark eyes.

She didn't look frightened, her gaze was fixed on her mother's face until those huge eyes slowly closed.

Lauren was smoothing the dark hair on the top of her little head. Lauren hoped it was comforting to Layla and she continued doing it until they reached the hospital even though the attendants told her Layla was gone. They gave her back to Lauren as they transported the two of them with a gurney. Lauren held her little lifeless body tightly. They wheeled the gurney into an emergency room to wait for the doctor to come.

"Are you ready for me to take her?" the nurse said. She could see from Lauren's face that she would never be ready.

"It's against the rules, but I think I can delay the doctor for a little while longer to give you time to say goodbye." The nurse chocked up, "I lost a baby once and I would have loved just a few more minutes."

"Thank you." Lauren said. "I will always remember this time. I love her so much!"

"*Just remember how this moment felt and she can be with you forever. Memorize how it feels to hold her and you can close your eyes and relive it.*" The nurse said, "*It will bring you some comfort in the days ahead.*" *She squeezed Lauren's hand and left the room.*

She purposely did not report directly to the doctor. She delayed a few minutes knowing it wasn't going to matter anyway.

When she saw the men from the morgue coming to claim the baby, she alerted the doctor that Lauren was ready.

"*I'll get the baby for you if you'll wait right here,*" *she told the men. She hoped it would be easier for Lauren to surrender the baby to her instead of the men who were strangers.*

She opened the door and saw Lauren rocking and singing softly to Layla, "*Amazing grace, how sweet the sound.*"

Tears started flowing down Lauren's cheeks as she realized why the nurse was back in the room.

"*Lauren,*" *she said hesitantly.* "*I'm so sorry, but it is time for Layla to leave. Would you let me take her?*" *Her voice was choking with emotion remembering how it felt when she had to give up her baby just a few short years ago.* "I promise you I will make sure she is handled carefully." The nurse added sympathetically.

"It's so hard," Lauren said in a whisper, "But I know she can't stay with me." She kissed the tiny forehead and handed her up to the nurse.

"I love you Layla. I will never forget you, I promise."

The nurse carefully held the tiny bundle close as she turned to leave the room. Behind her she heard the sobs begin, knowing there was nothing she could do to stop them. She left the room and closed the door behind her.

When Lauren's ER doctor came in to examine her, he decided her gynecologist needed to come see her yet that morning. He detected an abnormality in her uterus and wanted a specialist to decide what should be done. She would have to endure another examination and another ultrasound.

Lauren laid staring up at the ceiling as the specialist did his exam feeling completely numb.

"Mrs. Jones?" The specialist asked.

"My name is Lauren." She answered simply.

"Okay," the specialist started again. "Lauren, I hate to tell you this but your uterus has been damaged from the premature delivery. There is a large amount of scar tissue in your womb. This scar tissue could be the cause of the premature delivery. It is extensive and we will need to do surgery as soon as I can get access to an operating room. Part of the uterine wall has pulled away with the removal of the placenta. I am sorry to tell you, but a hysterectomy is the probable outcome of the surgery." The doctor paused. "Do you understand what I'm telling you?"

"If I don't have a uterus I will not be able to have another baby?" Lauren asked. "There's no other way?"

"I'm sorry," the doctor said sympathetically. "That is correct. There's too much damage and even if we can save your uterus, it is doubtful you would ever be able to support another pregnancy."

Lauren was lying alone on the gurney in the emergency room when Robert got there.

"You should have called me sooner. The prison just left a message on the answering machine, and I didn't get it until mid morning." Robert said defensively. "It was your fault I had to call the police, you know."

Lauren just laid there staring at the ceiling. She had neither the desire nor the strength to answer him.

"I see you're not going to talk to me. Fine, I'll leave. But I wanted you to know that I dropped the assault charges. . .you're welcome." She was glad to hear the door shut behind him.

Robert went out to the nurse's desk.

"She won't talk to me." Robert said to the nurse. "Has she had any visitors? I'm just checking to see if she can communicate."

"Let me check her records," she searched the screen of the computer. "Yes," she said. "I can give you information since you are on her medical records list." She reported back. "I show she has had three visitors, all three were doctors. One was her ER doctor, initials HT, another was her gynecologist specialist, and the other was an MD, with the initials GK. Only the ER doctor and the gynecologist made notations in her records. The MD was just visiting.

"Okay, if she's had visitors, she must be able to talk. I'll come back later after her surgery." Robert walked out of the reception area and out the front door. He had to find out how a person disposes of a premature baby's body. He didn't see why a funeral or service would be needed. After all, she only lived a few minutes.

"Hello?" It was the hospital Chaplin at her door. The nurse had suggested to him that he make a visit to Lauren.

He was a middle aged man wearing a black suit and white shirt. "Would you like to talk?"

"Yes I would." Lauren said. "I need help. I really need some body's help."

Chapter Twenty
Chemo-Week Number Nineteen

Monday mornings seemed to come around so quickly. It officially was two and one half months of this routine. Robert struggled to get up out of bed and it took everything he had just to walk to the bathroom. He held on to the furniture the whole way, not trusting his legs to support his body.

The taxi cab arrived and the driver was now directed to come to the door to help his fare out to the car. Robert had lost all of the muscle in his arms and legs. It had taken years of exercise to create his six pack abs but now they were gone, along with sixty pounds of weight. He was down to loose wrinkly skin and bones.

Maria met the taxi cab driver at the curb with a black and chrome wheel chair.

"How are you doing today?" She asked.

"As well as an eighty year old man can be," he answered.

She laughed, "Don't be so discouraged. It won't be long since you are already at week number nineteen. You are coming through this just fine." She patted his shoulder as she pushed the wheel chair into the waiting room bumping over the door ways and floor mats.

"Trust me," she said kindly. "You will recover your strength though you need to remember it usually takes longer to regain it then it does to lose it."

"Here's the pinch," Maria said as she inserted the needle expertly into his vein. He closed his eyes. It never used to bother him to get a shot but now he could barely stand to see the needle anywhere near his arm.

Lately he was having nightmares. He dreamed that Maria started having the same side effects as he did. Last night, he dreamed that she bent over and he could see the top of her head. It was totally bald! She only had hair left on the fringes. When she stood back up, chunks of her hair started falling out. They were dropping on the floor beside them in snarled clumps.

She came up close to his face and he could smell her perfume, but then he noticed her skin was all dry and flaky. Her eyes were sunken in so deep he could no longer tell if they were blue.

He woke up, drenched in sweat and was very nervous to come today. He had to see that she was still his pillar of strength, unaffected by the chemicals she handled.

He looked up at her sweet face as she filled the vials with blood. Thank goodness her skin was still soft and satiny. Her hair was still shiny and thick. He realized what he had known all along. He wasn't sure he could handle this ordeal without her.

Maria left to deliver the blood samples to the lab. Then they would have to have the okay from Dr. Kimball.

Robert sat looking through a magazine waiting for Maria to return to start his chemo.

"Mrs. Vaughn won't be coming any longer." Robert overheard the nurse say to the receptionist behind the desk. "She passed away last night."

"I'll remove her from our appointment schedule." The receptionist said without any emotion.

Robert was shocked. Was that how it worked? Nurses pretended to take care of you, but if you passed away they just removed you from the schedule? Did they throw away your file? Did they take your number out of the rolodex? Robert was upset to think he could die and they wouldn't even think twice about it. Would they miss him at all? Surely, Maria was different.

The thought of Mrs. Vaughn dying really disturbed him. He decided he would call and make an appointment with Doctor Kimball. It had been a couple of weeks since he had been seen and he wanted to see his charts. Hopefully he was making good progress by now. As soon as he got home he would call.

When Maria returned to the stark white room he asked about the elderly woman he now knew to be named Mrs. Vaughn.

"Such a shame, she seemed like a nice lady." She said simply.

"Was there a connection between you and her?" He asked. "Did you know her outside of the hospital?"

"No," she said thoughtfully. "I had never met her before she came here for her treatments. But if you are wondering if someone will be taking her place, I can assure you they will be scheduling in a new patient next week. You won't have to face your treatments alone."

Robert was stunned. Maria's bedside manner made him believe she really cared for the gray haired woman. Now he realizes she was just doing her job, putting on an act to try to comfort someone. He also realized she wouldn't be attending her funeral. They simply just schedule in a new person.

Would Maria be just as cavalier if it was he that died? He decided he'd really rather not think about it.

With that decided he could now relax and rest a while. Maria informed him that his test results had been sufficient. The cold of the chemo was now entering his veins.

Chapter Twenty One

The metal barrel felt comforting in his mouth. It tasted like gun powder and oil.

He removed it and looked down at the table beside him one more time and checked to make sure all of his papers were in order. He had his will, he had his life insurance policy with his alma mater as his beneficiary and he had the envelope on top addressed to the McKinley law firm.

As he bent over, his glasses slid down his nose and he used his index finger to push them back into place. What was the point? He took them off and laid them on top of the stack of papers.

He closed his eyes and imagined her face. He smiled even though her face had been so sad the last time he saw her. He raised the barrel to his mouth again, and sighed heavily. He squeezed the trigger.

When the shot rang out, the lady in the next apartment woke from a deep sleep terrified. She quickly called the police in a panic to report it.

A splatter of blood appeared across the stack of papers. After the body fell to the floor, the room was quiet.

Chapter Twenty Two
August 1978

Robert planned Layla's funeral since Lauren was recovering from her surgery. They did perform a hysterectomy, as expected.

Lauren was allowed to leave the hospital to attend the funeral. Robert brought her a black pantsuit to wear. He forgot to bring her shoes so her only choice was her white tennis shoes. Robert kept it simple and only invited the two of them.

When Lauren walked in the door of the funeral home and saw the tiny little casket her knees went weak and her heart ached for her baby. All she wanted to do is gather Layla up into her arms and run out of the door.

Lauren was upset that Robert did not have anyone coming to officiate. She decided her baby deserved a few words, and she realized it was up to her to do it.

"Layla, my tiny baby, I will love you forever." She stood in front of the casket swaying slightly from side to side. She had to be strong for Layla. "You will always be in my heart and my soul. I will see you again in heaven. Trust me, I will see you again."

She paused to sigh deeply and wipe away the tears flowing down her cheeks.

"I am so grateful to have had you, even if for only a short time." Her eyes were full of tears and her voice was so chocked up, it was hard to understand her.

"You are my tiny angel."

Robert carried her tiny casket out to the cemetery with the help of a man from the funeral home. Lauren walked behind them sobbing the entire way. Lauren kissed the top of the casket and laid a pale pink rose on the top. Her tomb stone said "Layla" and the words "Our tiny angel."

Robert said he needed to leave as soon as the funeral was over because he had a big business meeting on the east coast. He took Lauren back to the hospital and watched her until she was back inside the big double doors. Then he quickly put his car into drive and headed to the interstate.

He was already packed and his suitcase was in the back seat. He would have to push the speed limit as he drove to the airport. He knew rush hour traffic would be brutal and he could not miss his plane.

Lauren stepped inside the hospital entryway, but slipped quietly into the public restroom. She waited in the gray painted stall for several minutes until she was sure Robert was gone. She cautiously left the restroom and stood by the large sliding automatic doors. Finally she saw a yellow and black cab pull up to the curb to drop off an old man.

She walked as quickly as she could to the curb waving at the cab driver. He saw her and rolled down his window. She asked, "Is this cab taken?"

"No," the cabby said, "Jump in. Where are you going?" He looked at her and smiled. She looked like it had been a long day since she looked weak and exhausted. Maybe she was visiting an ill person at the hospital and had sat bedside for hours.

She gave him her house number and Cherry Hill Lane then slid into the back seat.

"Take me home," she said "Please just take me home." He locked in her house number and reset his meter to zero.

She did not speak during the long drive even though he kept trying to start a *conversation. He hated seeing someone look so terribly sad. She must have received very bad news and was very deep in thought. He realized she didn't even know he was talking to her. She was young enough to be his daughter and it broke his heart to think of someone so young being in such distress.*

When he got to her driveway, she paid him his fare. Finally she acknowledged him by looking him directly in his eyes and asked, "Would you please come back to get me in three hours? Would you please?"

She held out a $20.00 bill and he said he would come back, taking the money and tucking it in his shirt pocket.

He was about the age her father was when he died and had very kind brown eyes that crinkled when he smiled. She was sure he would come back to get her.

Lauren had secretly started to pack her bags a long time ago. She had two large dark grey suitcases hidden in her closet that were already packed full. She also had a list of last minute things that she couldn't pack until she was ready to leave so Robert wouldn't notice things were missing.

Robert would be surprised to find her gone. He thought of her as a puppet where he controlled the strings and every move she made. She had only been staying in the marriage for Layla's sake to ensure she had proper health care. Besides she did not have to deal with Robert every day since he was gone a lot of the time. She looked forward to his days on the road and was anxious and stressed for the days he spent at home.

This was the day, the day of freedom. Robert would be in California for four days, so she could get far away before he realized she was gone.

She got the heavy suitcases out of the closet and dragged them to the door, setting them side by side like soldiers waiting at attention.

Out from under the bed came the two flattened cardboard boxes. She saved them from the delivery of their new furniture. The roll of packing tape was carefully hidden in her cosmetic case.

She urgently taped the boxes into symmetrical strong cubes. She got her purse, where she kept the list in a small zippered compartment.

Methodically, she gathered the items from the list and placed them into the box. She located the kitchen curtains she had sewn from the box marked 'shoes' in her closet. They would be displayed in a future *home free from Robert and his lopsided ideals.*

Some items got wrapped in the newspaper she saved in the recycle bin in the pantry. Each item resulted in a red check mark on the list.

She went to get the picture of her parents she kept in the drawer of the night stand beside her bed. She had wanted to display it, but Robert wouldn't stand for it. Instead she kept it in the drawer and got it out when she needed comfort and he was out of town.

She wished more than anything that her parents would still be alive. That drunk driver not only took her parents but affected her life as well. They would have been glad to have her come live with them and would have been thrilled at the idea of her having a baby. At least she could have had their support at Layla's funeral. They would have understood how devastated she was.

Robert sure didn't.

Thank goodness she had the pastor and the people at the shelter to rely on because otherwise she was totally alone in this world.

She packed the small sack full of things purchased for Layla. Layla and her mother formed a bond from the day she knew she was pregnant. These small items, booties, sleepers and layettes were meant for Layla, so they would not stay behind for Robert to throw away.

She worked feverishly until every item had a red check mark beside it on the list. From time to time she sat down to res since she felt so weak. Her surgery took away the majority of her strength, but none of her determination to leave.

There was only one item left on the list. The painting was the only battle she had ever won in this household. It was a beautiful picture of a sunset entitled, <u>"There Is Always Another Day."</u>

Robert wanted a picture of himself standing by his Mercedes to hang above the fireplace. It was so important for Robert to brag on his success even in his own home.

Lauren had always appreciated the work of an artist. In a photo, the picture was what happened in one small moment of time that a photographer was lucky enough to catch. In an artist painting, every brush stroke, every color choice, and every detail were choices made by the artist to tell their story. This makes artwork a skill to be respected.

She often would sit and admire this painting and would try to imagine what the artist was thinking when she chose to tint the water with turquoise, or how she chose to show shadows on the trees as they bent over the lake.   Every time she studied the painting she found a new detail, added by the artist with a specific reason in mind.

"What is that painting?" Robert asked when he saw it hanging above the fireplace. "It looks like a dumb sunset. I don't like it," he said firmly. Lauren took the painting from her parent's house before the estate sale. She had always admired it in their home. But she knew how to work this with Robert to get her way.

"Actually, "she said coming directly to the point.   "It is a VERY expensive 'dumb' sunset. Your friends would be very impressed when they see the artist's signature and realize how much this painting is worth."

Robert looked thoughtful for a moment then nodded his head and said, "I see your point. It belongs over the mantle where everyone can see it."

Lauren would often sit on the couch and stare up at the painting. It was a lie. It was not an expensive painting but Lauren loved it. The sunset was not an ending for her. To her it said this day is now over but tomorrow is always a fresh start. It is the promise of a happy future. And that is why it needed to go with her on her journey.

The ladder seemed to want to stay in the garage. It fought her every step of the way. When she tried to get it off of the big hooks on the wall, it kept catching at the top, refusing to let go. With a big thrust upwards it finally came down with a large crash on the cement floor beside her hooks and all. Oh well, she had no intention of ever trying to put it back up on that hook anyhow.

As she carried it up the two step entry way it caught on the step. She lifted it higher and it caught on the door frame above. Finally it made it to stand in front of the mantle.

She was very frustrated from her struggle with the ladder. Sweat was beaded up on her forehead. She wore her hair in a blonde ponytail tied with a snip of black ribbon. She did it to defy Robert, since he no longer wanted her to wear her hair this way. He thought it was too juvenile for a woman of status.

She climbed up the ladder, with her legs shaking the whole way. She made it to the third step and tried to take the painting down. The end of the frame on her side came free but the corner on the far end was caught on the nail. She shifted it back and forth, climbed up another rung and leaned farther forward but it still refused to come loose.

She climbed up another step, panting from her efforts, and tried a quick jerk upward to free the painting from its nail. The painting suddenly came free causing her to lose her balance. Down she fell, face down between the ladder and the fireplace. Her hips hit the carpeted floor first but her chin hit the stone hearth and her head snapped backwards violently.

She must have passed out. When she opened her eyes her first thought was she didn't feel any pain except for her chin and jaw. She'd probably have a huge scrape under her chin, but at least it was from her own stupidity instead of from Robert's anger.

Her hand was stretched out, palm flat on the floor not far from her face. The painting landed right side up leaning against the couch, displaying its beauty to her, but blocking out the view of the rest of the room.

All she could see was her hand and the setting sun. She braced her hand to try to get up, but her hand and arm did not respond.

"What is wrong with me?" She thought. She tried to lift her fingers, one at a time, but they would not respond to her commands. She tried to move her legs, her feet and her toes with no results. When she tried to lift her head it caused a searing pain that shot up the back of her neck.

Maybe if she stayed still for a while her limbs would respond. Maybe she was just tired or in shock. Surely this was all temporary and she'd soon make the call to the woman's shelter the Pastor told her about. All she had to do is call and they would tell her where to meet them. Then they would take her to the shelter and she would be safe until she could make other arrangements.

She was so close to freedom, all she had to do is get out of that front door.

She calmed herself down and thought time might be her cure. She focused on the painting so she wouldn't panic again.

She concentrated on the brush strokes, "Why were some brush strokes vertical while others were horizontal?" She noticed that the center of the sun, just where it disappeared behind the trees, had brush strokes going at angles instead of up and down. How come she had never noticed that *before? In fact they swirled around and created an oval, an oval with extra texture and very specific colors blended in. She realized it created a face, a small, perfect little face with huge dark eyes. The eyes looked directly at hers as they had once before. Lauren's eyes filled with tears and the drops blurred her vision. She had to blink many times to clear the tears so she could see the tiny face in front of her.*

It was Layla.

Chapter Twenty Three

Joan looked at the clock one more time. It was 3:15 on Friday afternoon. She was casually dressed in a faded T-shirt and jeans. Her job often required carrying suitcases, carrying babies or small children and sometimes a pet or two. Whatever a family decides it needed to survive.

She had grown many gray hairs from cases that ended in potential violence. She even had an abused Mom held hostage and she had to involve the state police to save her.

She was starting to get very worried. Why did she get so involved with these cases? Why did she care so much? It led to many sleepless nights and anxious days of waiting. When people contacted this refuge for help she tried to remove them from their situation as quickly as possible. But Lauren had told the Pastor she couldn't leave until after her daughter's funeral. That was on Tuesday, this was Friday. Poor lady, it was a week that would be any parent's nightmare.

Joan could do nothing but sit and wait for the call. Unfortunately her intuition told her that something was wrong, horribly wrong.

The only information she had was the woman was in jail for assault and was transported to the city hospital. On the way there she lost her baby. She was terribly afraid of her husband and needed to find a safe place to go. Normally Joan could not contact the people they heard from. They could only wait for the call that someone was ready for help.

Not trying to contact them was to protect the abused person too. If protective services called the house and the abuser answered the phone, it could cause a chain reaction of violence. Unfortunately, this sometimes happened no matter how hard they tried.

Chapter Twenty Four
Chemo-Week Number Twenty

Robert called Dr. Gene Kimball's office to make an appointment.
"Hello?" The receptionist asked.
"This is Robert Jones. I'm a patient of Dr. Kimball. I need to make an appointment as soon as he can see me."
"Mr. Jones," the receptionist said. "I'm not going to be able to make that appointment. You have been reassigned to Dr. Hubble."
"No," Robert said insistently. "Dr. Kimball takes care of my case personally. I only want to see him."
"I'm sorry, that will not be possible," the receptionist answered. "Dr. Kimball is no longer with us."
"He moved to another hospital?" Robert asked confused.
"No," she answered. "He is dead. He committed suicide a few days ago."
Robert was stunned. Could his luck get any worse? Having his treatment personally supervised by a specialist meant a lot to him. It made him feel like he had a

better chance at surviving this with the expertise of a specialist. Now he would have to start over with someone new.
	"An appointment with Dr. Hubble will be okay, but I need to be seen as soon as possible." Robert said defeated.

Chapter Twenty Five
August 1978

Joan decided to contact the Pastor.

"Hello?" He answered his phone.

"Pastor," she explained. "This is Joan from the East Side Woman's Shelter. I have not received a call from Lauren, the woman from the hospital you called me about."Do you think you could check on her for me since you are her contact?"

"You haven't heard anything from her?" He asked surprised. "Joan, I think we have a problem. Thank you for calling me." The concern was clearly heard in his voice. I am going to head to the hospital right now to see if she is still there. I'll call you as soon as I know something."

Joan sat down to wait. She spent so much time waiting to hear and hoping the news would not be bad news.

Joan and the pastor had worked together on several cases before. They both cared way too much about the people they worked with. Unfortunately, they both had seen cases that ended in tragedy.

The Pastor arrived at the hospital in a yellow and black cab. "I hate seeing a Pastor going to the hospital. Are you giving last rites to a patient?" the cab driver asked.

"Hopefully not," the Pastor said. "Hopefully I can save someone this time."

"Well, I hope you will have better luck with patients from this hospital than I have been having this week." The cabbie said. . "I got stood up on Tuesday with someone I picked up here"."

"What do you mean?" answered the Pastor. "Stood up? At a hospital?"

"Actually I picked her up here and she looked so terribly sad. I took her to her home and she asked me to come back in three hours. She said it was very important. She was such a sad young lady." He scratched the back of his head.

"I believed her when she gave me the twenty as a tip. I stopped by several times and honked. I even went to the door once but she never came out even though her lights were on. I guess she got another ride, though that would have been a waste of her twenty."

This caught the Pastor's attention. "Her lights were on but she didn't come to the door? Did she have a long blonde hair, medium build?" The cabbie nodded. The pastor thought for a moment, "Can you wait for me?" He asked the cabbie. "If my patient is gone, I'll bet that was her you gave a ride to."

The Pastor opened the car door and ran into the hospital and up to the reception desk. He explained his situation and the supervisor came out to talk to him.

"Yes," the supervisor said. "She had a hysterectomy and headed to her daughters funeral on Tuesday but she never returned as she was scheduled to. "

"Thank you!" The Pastor said and he headed out to the cab that was still waiting by the curb.

"Do you remember where you took the young lady?" He said through the open window. Again the cabbie nodded yes and off they sped toward Lauren's house.

"Cherry Hill Lane. There's the house. See the lights are still on," the cab driver said.

"Thank you," the pastor said and he got out of the cab and jogged up the driveway to the front door.

The cab driver parked and was right behind him. They knocked on the front door and received no answer. The glass on the front door was a beautiful etched pattern. Unfortunately they couldn't see through I clearly.

The Pastor went around the side of the house to a side window. The cab driver gave him a boost so he could see into the living room.

He could see a ladder lying on its side on the floor in front of the fireplace. He could also see a large wooden square leaning against the couch. He wasn't sure what it was. Panic ran through him and the hair on his arms bristled when he realized there was a pair of tennis shoes lying soles upward on the floor.

His eyes were growing accustomed to the dark and he could make out legs covered with black slacks sticking out from behind the grey recliner. He rang the door bell a few more times and then started to bang on the front door in frustration.

A neighbor asked from the sidewalk, "Can I help you?" as he walked his dog down the sidewalk.

"Yes!" The Pastor said. "Call 911 and hurry!!"

Robert was in the airport since he arrived home earlier than he expected. He had been on standby in Boston and was surprised to hear his name called for a seat. Normally stand by never seemed to work out for him. He wanted this flight because a woman he met at the convention told him she was on this flight. She mentioned she needed to get a cab ride home from the airport.

He decided he could offer her a ride home since his car was at the airport. This is why he was so excited to get a seat on this flight. She graciously accepted his offer for a ride. On the way home they stopped at a cozy little bar just outside the city limits.

He had a few hours of free time and he was determined to enjoy it.

Chapter Twenty Six

The police pulled up in front of the house on Cherry Hill Lane. Unfortunately this was not their first visit to the residence. This time the call was from a neighbor who said a Pastor told him to make the 911 call. There was concern about a woman that lived there.

Sergeant Wilson hoped it wasn't the blond that he took to jail for slapping her husband. That whole situation still bothered him. He was sure there was much more to that story than it appeared on the surface and did not trust the husband at all. But he did what the rules said he had to do. He had no choice.

The Pastor came running over to the police car as soon as they pulled into the driveway.

"I can see someone lying on the floor but I knocked on the door and she's not answering or moving," the Pastor said.
"I'm afraid we may find the worst."

Roberts plan had worked out nicely. He really enjoyed Diane's company and she listened intently to all of his stories about how successful he was.

She was very sympathetic when he explained to her that his wife didn't understand him and that nothing he did was ever good enough for her. He told her about their beautiful house, her expensive clothes and jewelry, and how he couldn't please her no matter what he did.

Diane's eyes widened as Robert described a huge diamond necklace that he gave Lauren as a gift but she thought was impractical. She wanted to return it after he had worked so hard to buy it for her. Okay, he had to admit that this one was a lie but the description of the huge diamond got Diane to agree to a second date on Saturday night. Robert definitely saw no problem with lying to get what he wanted, a game he was determined to win over and over.

As he guided his Mercedes around the corner and turned down his block he saw dozens of flashing lights. As he got closer he saw the two police cars and the ambulance were in his driveway! He stopped breathing for a few seconds when he saw the EMT's wheeling a gurney up the side walk to his front door.

He pulled up by the curb and rolled down his window. "That's my house!" He yelled to the officers whose cars were barricading the driveway. The officer flagged him in. Robert threw his car into park and headed up the sidewalk.

"What happened?" He yelled hysterically. "What happened? Is my house damaged?"

The officer at the door asked him if he could see some identification. "Damn you!" Robert yelled. "This is MY house! Did someone break in?"

"Sir," the officer said trying to calm him. "What is your name?"

"I'm Robert Jones," he said. "And this is MY house!" He pulled out his billfold displaying his license to prove it. "What has happened?"

"Sir," the police officer said returning the billfold now satisfied. "Who lives here with you?"

"My wife Lauren, but she's in the hospital." He said confused. "Anyway I think she still is. I guess I'm not sure. I've been out of town for the last four days."

"Well, I'm sorry to tell you that we just found a woman dead on your living room floor. We will need you to identify her." He paused. "It may or may not be your wife."

"Dead? My wife?" Robert said shocked. "That's impossible. She's at the hospital." He had been too busy at the conference and he did not try to call her all week. He didn't want to hear her cry over the baby. He figured she'd be calmed down and back to normal by the time he got home.

When they got inside they saw the woman was already in a body bag on the gurney. Investigators had already photographed the scene and collected evidence in case foul play would be suspected. The officer stopped the ambulance attendants as they wheeled the gurney toward the front door.

"Can you unzip for identification?" The attendant nodded and started tugging on the massive zipper. He folded back the flap of black vinyl to expose the face inside.

Lauren's green eyes were open wide and her face was twisted to the side. Rigor mortis had frozen it in place. Her neck was discolored bright purple where the blood from her injury had pooled.

"That's Lauren," he said in disbelief. "That's my wife. Do you know what happened?"

"It appears she fell off of a ladder and hit her head on the fireplace hearth." The officer reported. "Were you moving? It appears she had her suitcases packed." He gestured toward the cases sitting by the front door and the two boxes taped tightly shut.

"NO!" Robert said defiantly. "We were NOT moving. I have no idea what she was doing. I thought she was still in the hospital."

"I do," a voice said breaking the silence. "I know what she was doing." And the Pastor stood up out of the shadows where he was sitting on the couch and walked up to them.

"You're just like she told me you were." He said and turned to the officer. "She was packing to leave him and come to our battered woman's shelter." He looked over by the fireplace. "She must have decided to take that picture with her when she left."

"Well, I can't imagine why you would tell such lies." Robert protested. "She would never leave me. I gave her everything. And if *she was taking that picture it was because it was very expensive,"* he shook his head slowly. *"She must have wanted to pawn it."*

Robert pointed at the Pastor. *"You're wrong!"* He said. *"She wouldn't have ever left me. She couldn't survive without me!"*

The Pastor stared Robert straight in the eye. *"I've heard that song and dance before."* And he turned and hurried out of the front door. He knew Robert would not be charged with anything. He had been gone most of the week and could prove it. There was nothing the Pastor could do for Lauren now. He felt so helpless having lost someone that asked for his help. He felt that he had let her down. He sighed deeply. He knew it would be another restless and sleepless night.

As he zipped back up the vinyl body bag the EMT explained to Robert that the preliminary cause of death was severe trauma to her neck and head. Unfortunately, his findings showed that she probably laid there for up to 48 hours before dying. She would have floated in and out of consciousness the whole time. Though, she wouldn't have been in a lot of pain due to her spinal cord injury.

"Thank you for everything you have done for my wife." Robert expressed his appreciation to the ambulance crew as they were leaving his house.

"We have everything we need for evidence. Our sympathy to you." The police officers said as they followed down the driveway. Sergeant Wilson also felt as if he had let Lauren down. His instincts had told him he could believe her. If only she hadn't slapped her husband. This would have turned out so differently.

Within a few minutes all of the rescue units had turned off their flashing warning lights and were heading down the street. Everything was quiet and dark again.

Robert shut the door behind them, shut off the front door entry lights and sank into the nearest chair. How could she do this to him after everything he did for her? The suitcases proved she was leaving. He would have to unpack them tomorrow to see if she was stealing other valuables of his.

He dressed for bed feeling numb and brushed his teeth. He'd have to go to the mortuary in the morning and make arrangements for his second funeral in a week. But tonight there was nothing he could do but sleep.

He crawled into bed and got settled and comfortable pulling the blankets up close to his chin. Suddenly he opened his eyes and thought, "Did I remember to mail it?"

He thought back and realized, yes, he had. Her life insurance payment would have been received on time.

Chapter Twenty Seven

"Hello," the short stout man said. "I am Dr. Hubble. Dr. Dwane Hubble." He offered his hand for Robert to shake. He was so glad this was his last appointment of the day. He was exhausted and knew it had been a long day from the amount of grey stubble on his chin. He straightened his light blue tie and sat down on the stool.

"Jones, Robert Jones," he said. "It's nice to meet you. Thank you for seeing me on such short notice."

"Well," the Doctor said hesitantly. "I've been anxious to talk to you since I received your latest blood samples and your records." He looked at Robert and started to explain.

"In some ways I have very good news for you. After testing your blood samples and reviewing your x-rays I am not finding any traces of liver cancer."

"That's wonderful!! I'm cured!!" Robert said delighted. "At least the hell I've gone through with these chemo treatments has been worth it! I feel like they've cost me my whole world. I've lost my house, my job, my Mercedes and I may still have to go bankrupt if I can't find a job soon. At least it was all worth it and I will live!!" Robert had not had this big of a smile on his face for a very long time.

"Robert," Dr. Hubble said patiently holding his hand up to quiet him. "You don't understand what I'm trying to tell you." Again he paused and swallowed hard.

"I'm not sure what Dr. Kimball was looking at in your test results, but when I say I can't find any signs of your cancer, I mean I'm not sure you EVER had any signs of liver cancer."

"No signs of having cancer? What are you talking about?" Robert questioned, thinking of all of the misery he has been through.

"He made a mistake? He misread an x-ray? Is that what you're trying to tell me? Robert froze. He looked hard at the Doctor. "Are you saying I did not need to go through chemotherapy?"

"Unfortunately, yes." Dr. Hubble said. "He made a mistake or he must have misread something for him to order such potent chemotherapy for you. Nothing else makes any sense. Because he handled your case personally no one else had access to your records or your lab test results. And now that he has passed away we may never know what he was thinking. I'm very sorry." He ran his hand over his balding head in frustration.

" I also have to tell you that you have liver damage from the high concentrations of chemo and you will need to be put on a liver transplant list to receive a donor liver. Again, I'm sorry to have to give you this information."

"If he was alive, Dr. Kimball would be the one that would be sorry. I've lost my whole life because of the chemo!" Robert was getting mad, very hot steaming mad.
His fists were clenched and the vein was popping out on the side of his face.

"He told me I needed to increase the dosages because he wasn't getting the results he wanted. The higher doses were horrible! I'm skin and bone! I've lost everything!" Robert stormed out of the office. "You'll hear from my lawyer!"

Robert aimlessly drove around for hours. He now drove a black Chevy Impala. It wasn't even a new one, it was six years old, but it was all he could afford after they repossessed his Mercedes.

He found himself driving to the old neighborhood on Cherry Hill Lane. He stopped along the curb across from his old house. It still looked very impressive. It was the image that he wanted to portray. He always loved the front entryway with its massive columns and crystal etched glass doors. The front entryway told everyone that someone of importance lived there.

He so wished he could move back into that house with Lauren. He wished he could have his furniture and his Mercedes back. That was a good time of life.

Now he lived in a three room apartment, with stark white painted walls. The owner of the building strictly forbids repainting so he had no choice but to live in it the way it was. Robert was left with very little furniture. It was like he had been forced back to the beginning of his career.

Finally he headed back to his apartment, resigned to the fact that he would have to start over.

The next morning he brewed himself a cup of coffee and had a seat at the old dining room table. He noticed a red flashing light on his answering machine telling him he had a message. He mindlessly pushed the button and listened for the response.

"This message is for Robert Jones. This is the office of McKinley Law Firm." The monotonous recorded voice continued.

"We are handling the will of Dr. Gene Kimball and he has left something for you. Please contact George McKinley at this office to make an appointment. #555-783-1110."

Robert listened to it three times before he was convinced he had the message down correctly.

Chapter Twenty-Eight

The McKinley Law Firm was in a huge high rise building downtown. The front entryway had a huge glass and brass revolving door with piped in classical music in the lobby. The interior smelled like fresh floor wax and money. Every person wore wool suits that rivaled Roberts very best.

He walked across the dark marble floors toward the woman sitting behind the huge maple desk. The desk top had a placard that said 'APPOINTMENTS.'

"Excuse me," Robert asked the young lady. "I have an appointment with George McKinley?"

"If you'll take a seat, I will let him know you are here." The lady didn't even look up at him with any interest at all. Since his chemo treatments woman looked through him, not at him.

When he receives his liver transplant he will show them, he will work hard to recover his strength and muscle. Maria told him that the first improvement he would see would be his hair growing back in. He couldn't wait.

"Robert Jones?" The distinguished gray haired man asked. "I am George McKinley. Thank you for coming in. Would you please follow me to my office?"

They shook hands and walked around the receptionist and down a short stretch of hallway. Mr. McKinley opened the huge double walnut doors and walked inside gesturing for Robert to follow.

The office was massive with a huge walnut desk and a very overstated black leather chair. The lawyer's desk top was made of marble and was completely empty except for a manila folder.

George McKinley sat down behind his desk.

"Have a seat, Mr. Jones." And Robert settled into an arm chair tufted with a velvet fabric. Robert was impressed to have his appointment with the owner of the firm. He must be very good at practicing law to have an office and a building like this.

"Mr. Jones," He looked at Robert squarely. "Do you remember Dr. Gene Kimball?" He opened the folder as he spoke.

"Yes, I do. He was my doctor before he died." Robert said. "What is this all about?"

"Well," the lawyer paused to pick up a long ivory envelope. "I have been instructed by Dr. Kimball's will to give this envelope to you. It is sealed so I have no idea what it contains, and it is up to you if you want to open it now or after you leave my office."

"I'll open it now," Robert said. "It's probably an apology or a cash award since I have recently discovered that Dr. Kimball made a mistake in handling my health care. He knows if he was still alive, he would be facing a huge malpractice lawsuit."

"He's lucky he donated all of\his money and life insurance proceeds to his alma mater a few weeks before he died or I would be suing his estate for all its worth." Robert continued, "As it is, there is nothing left to sue for."

Robert read the front of the envelope. It said George McKinley's name plus the instruction, 'For Robert Jones-confidential.' He noticed the brown splatters across the names. He decided not to ask what they were.

He quickly slid his index finger under the envelope flap. The first thing he saw was a photograph. He pulled it out and looked at it. The photograph was wrinkled and quite worn around the edges.

It was a picture of a young man with large dark framed glasses and a young lady with blonde hair fashioned into a pony tail. She was wearing a rust colored dress that fit snugly at her waist and accented her green eyes and her olive skin. Stamped on the corner of the picture was the fraternity symbol for Sigma Nu.

They were standing side by side and the boy was sheepishly holding her hand and looking at her instead of looking at the photographer. The look on his face was unmistakable.

"What the…" Robert said as he realized who the people in the picture were. He quickly tore the envelope open to see what else was inside.

It was a small square of paper, about a quarter of a sheet. It was a letter hand written in ink. It said:

Because of my love for Lauren.

Made in the USA
Lexington, KY
26 February 2017